W9-BWU-629

Sassafrass, Cypress & Indigo

St.

Martin's

Press

New

York

Sassafrass, Cypress & Indigo

a novel by

Ntozake Shange

Design by Cynthia Krupat

Library of Congress Cataloging in Publication Data
Shange, Ntozake.
  Sassafras, Cypress & Indigo.
  I. Title.   II. Title: Sassafras, Cypress, and
Indigo.
PS3569.H3324S2   813'.54   82–5565
ISBN 0–312–69971–9   AACR2

10 9 8 7 6 5 4 3

Sassafrass,
Cypress &
Indigo
is dedicated to
all women
in struggle.

ACKNOWLEDGMENTS

*This book was made possible by
grants from The Solomon Guggenheim
Foundation, The New York State
Council on the Arts, The National
Endowment for the Arts, and the
MacDowell Colony.*

*I thank Bonnie Daniels, who
unfailingly assisted me with the varied
manuscripts that became the novel. I
must also thank my editor, Michael
Denneny, for believing the novel was
lingering in my soul.*

Sassafrass, Cypress & Indigo

*W*here there is a woman there is magic. If there is a moon falling from her mouth, she is a woman who knows her magic, who can share or not share her powers. A woman with a moon falling from her mouth, roses between her legs and tiaras of Spanish moss, this woman is a consort of the spirits.

Indigo seldom spoke. There was a moon in her mouth. Having a moon in her mouth kept her laughing. Whenever her mother tried to pull the moss off her head, or clip the roses round her thighs, Indigo was laughing.

"Mama, if you pull 'em off, they'll just grow back. It's my blood. I've got earth blood, filled up with the Geechees long gone, and the sea."

Sitting among her dolls, Indigo looked quite mad. As a small child, she stuffed socks with red beans, raw rice, sawdust or palm leaves. Tied ribbons made necks, so they could have heads and torsos. Then eyes from carefully chosen buttons or threads, hair from yarns specially dyed by her sisters and her mama, dresses of the finest silk patches, linen shoes and cotton underskirts, satin mitts or gloves embroidered with the delight of a child's hand. These creatures were still her companions, keeping pace with her changes, her moods and dreams, as no one else could. Indigo heard them talking to her in her sleep. Sometimes when someone else was talking, Indigo excused herself—her dolls were calling for her. There was so much to do. Black people needed so many things. That's why Indigo didn't tell her mama what all she discussed with her friends. It had nothing to do with Jesus. Nothing at all. Even her mama knew that, and she would shake her head the way folks do when they hear bad news, murmuring, "Something's got hold to my child, I swear. She's got too much South in her."

The South in her, the land and salt-winds, moved her through Charleston's streets as if she were a mobile sapling, with the gait of a well-loved colored woman whose lover was the horizon in any direction. Indigo imagined tough winding branches growing from her braids, deep green leaves rustling by her ears, doves and macaws flirting above the nests they'd fashioned in the secret, protected niches way high up in her headdress. When she wore this Carolinian costume, she knew the cobblestone streets were really polished oyster shells, covered with pine needles and cotton flowers. She made herself, her world, from all that she came from. She looked around her at the wharf. If there was nobody there but white folks, she made them black folks. In the grocery, if the white folks were buying up all the fresh collards and okra, she made them disappear and put the produce on the vegetable wagons that went round to the Colored. There wasn't enough for Indigo in the world she'd been born to, so she made up what she needed. What she thought the black people needed.

Access to the moon.
The power to heal.
Daily visits with the spirits.

MOON JOURNEYS
cartography by Indigo

Find an oval stone that's very smooth. Wash it in rosewa-
ter, 2 times. Lay it out to dry in the night air where no
one goes. When dry, hold stone tightly in the right hand,
caress entire face with the left hand. Repeat the same
action with the stone in the left hand. Without halting
the movement, clasp left stone-filled hand with the right.
Walk to a tree that houses a spirit-friend. Sit under the
tree facing the direction of your mother's birthplace.
Hold your hands between your bosom, tight. Take 5
quick breaths and 3 slow ones. Close your eyes. You are
on your way.

ALTERNATIVE MODES OF
MOON JOURNEYS
(Winter travel/Inclement weather)

In a thoroughly cleaned bathroom with the window open,
burn magnolia incense, preferably, but cinnamon will
do. In a handkerchief handled by some other woman in
your family (the further back the better), put chamomile,
an undamaged birthwort leaf, and Lady's Fern. Tie this
with a ribbon from your own hair. Kiss the sachet 3
times. Drop it gently into a tub of warm water that will
cover all your body. Place two white burning candles at
either end of the tub. Float one fully opened flower in
the water. Get in the tub while tickling the water in
circles with the petals of the flower. Lie in the tub, with

5/

flower over your heart. Close your eyes. You are on your way.

Not all black people wanted to go to the moon. But some did. Aunt Haydee had gone to the moon a lot. She'd told Indigo about the marvelous parties there were in the very spots the white people put flags and jumped up and down erratically. They never did learn how to dance. Been round black folks all these years and still don't have sense enough to keep in rhythm. But there they were walking on the moon, like nothing ever went on up there. Like women didn't sidle up to lunar hills every month. Like seas of menses could be held back by a rocket launcher. Like the Colored might disappear with the light of the moon.

"We ain't goin' anywhere, are we?" Indigo sat some of the dolls on the inside of her thigh. Her very favorites she sat in her lap. Indigo had made every kind of friend she wanted. African dolls filled with cotton root bark, so they'd have no more slave children. Jamaican dolls in red turbans, bodies formed with comfrey leaves because they'd had to work on Caribbean and American plantations and their bodies must ache and be sore. Then there were the mammy dolls that Indigo labored over for months. They were almost four feet high, with big gold earrings made from dried sunflowers, and tits of uncleaned cotton. They smelled of fennel, peach leaves, wild ginger, wild yams. She still crawled up into their arms when she was unavoidably lonely, anxious that no living black folks would talk to her the way her dolls and Aunt Haydee did.

Everybody said she was just too ornery to hold a decent conversation. But that wasn't true. What was true was that Indigo had always had to fight Cypress and Sassafrass just to get them to listen to her. They thought they were so grown. So filled up with white folks' ways. They didn't want to hear about the things Aunt Haydee knew. Indigo watched her mother over huge vats of dyes, carrying newly spun yarn from the pots to the lines and back again. Sassafrass, throwing shuttles back and forth and back and forth. Cypress tying off cloth, carrying the cloth to the stairway where she began the appliqués the family was famous for. There was too much back and forth going on for anybody to engage little Indigo in conversations about the haints and the Colored. If the rhythm was interrupted, Sassafrass would just stare at the loom. Cypress would look at her work and not know where to start or what gauge her stitches were. Mama would burn herself with some peculiarly tinted boiling water. Everybody would be mad and not working, so Indigo was sent to talk to the dolls. All the dolls in the house became hers. And the worlds Sassafrass wandered in her weaving, and those Cypress conjured through her body, were lost to Indigo, who handled three-way conversations with her cloth companions all alone.

A girl-child with her dolls is unlikely to arouse attention anywhere, same as little boys with footballs or Davy Crockett hats. So Indigo would sneak from the place she'd been put (the corridor around the back porch), and take her friends out visiting. Old ladies loved for Indigo and Company to pass by. They would give her homemade butter cookies or gingerbread. They offered teas and chocolates, as well as the Scriptures and the legends of their lives. Indigo only had colored dolls and only visited colored ladies. She didn't like Miz Fitzhugh, who fawned over Cypress and Sassafrass like they were 'most white. No, Mrs. Yancey with the low, secret voice and seventeen million hundred braids was Indigo's friend. And Sister Mary Louise who kept a garden of rose bushes and herbs was Indigo's cut-buddy, down to the Colored Methodist Episcopal Church.

Streets in Charleston wind the way old ladies' fingers crochet as they unravel the memories of their girlhoods. One thing about a Charlestonian female is her way with little things. The delicacy of her manner. The force of ritual in her daily undertakings. So what is most ordinary is made extraordinary. What is hard seems simple. Indigo listened to their tales, the short and long ones, with a mind to make herself a doll whose story that was, or who could have helped out. When her father died, Indigo had decided it was the spirit of things that mattered. The humans come and go. Aunt Haydee said spirits couldn't be gone, or the planet would fall apart.
The South in her.

Rumor was that Mrs. Yancey had a way with white folks. They couldn't deny her anything. That's what folks said . . . that she must honey up to them; leastways, smile a lot. That was the only way the beautiful things she had in her house could be accounted for. Mrs. Yancey couldn't have bought such lace, or that silver tea service. Imagine a colored woman having afternoon tea and crumpets with all that silver. Indigo always carried her doll-friend Miranda over to Mrs. Yancey's. Miranda had better manners than some of her other dolls. Miranda was always clean, too, in a red paisley pinafore and small black sandals. Indigo let Miranda use her parasol to protect her from the sun. What proper young woman would come visiting faint and perspiring? Only some of Indigo's more country dolls would have marched to Mrs. Yancey's with the outdoors all over them.

Indigo walked up to Mrs. Yancey's front porch, pulled her slip up, and fussed with the hair sticking out of her braids. She'd rinsed her hands off, but re-doing her hair for a short chat seemed to make too much of a regular outing. Besides, Miranda was really dressed up. Indigo had decorated her bonnet with dandelions, and sprayed some of her mama's perfume under her arms and behind her knees. When she was ready, Indigo rang the bell and waited. Sure enough, Mrs. Yancey was coming to the door. She wore slippers with the heels all beat down that made a sound like Bill Bojangles when he did the soft shoe. Opening the bright white door, while pulling the apron from around her neck, Mrs. Yancey bent down to kiss Indigo on the cheek.

"Now ain't you looking mighty fresh today, Indigo. And Miranda must be going to a social, all decked out, huh?"

"No, M'am. We just thought you might want some company. I was talking to Miranda and she told me you were thinking on us real hard."

"Y'all come in and make yourselves at ease in the parlor. Miranda must gotta second sense. She always knows when I wanna see my little girls."

Mrs. Yancey's house smelled like collard greens and corn bread, even when she fried oysters and made red sauce. Indigo nudged Miranda.

"Can ya smell that? Mrs. Yancey's house smells good, doesn't it?" Her house felt good, too. There were so many soft places to sit and smell other things. Mrs. Yancey liked to make pillows. Oval pillows, square pillows, rectangles, triangles, shapes that had no names but were scented, soft, huggable pillows. These pillows were covered with satins and silks, and embroidered in blinding scarlets and golds, and set off with laces, tassels, and cords. Mrs. Yancey told Miranda that she made the pillows now because all her life she had been living between a rock and a hard place. Even though she didn't really need any more, something called her to keep sewing herself comforts. Miranda asked Mrs. Yancey the questions that Indigo considered too forward. Why, one time when Miranda and Indigo were having a bit of pineapple-upside-down cake with their tea, and Mrs. Yancey was talking about how the white folks drove down the Colored, drove the Colored to drink and evil ways, drove decent young gals into lives of sin, chasing them up and down the back stairways from Allendale to Hilton Head, Miranda blurted:

"Well, how come the white people give you so many things? If they so hard-hearted and low-down, why you smile up to 'em?"

Indigo was embarrassed, and gave Miranda a good whack 'cross the face.

"She didn't mean that, M'am."

"Yes, she did, Indigo. She did, and it ain't correct to be slapping on no free somebody. You keep your hands to yourself and listen to what I gotta say."

Indigo settled back in the love seat, almost disappearing in all the pillows. Miranda finally relaxed and lay next to her, listening.

"Folks in these parts got sucha low idea of the women of the race. They can't imagine how I come by what I come by 'less they weigh my reputation down with they dirty, filthy minds."

"Oh, no M'am, didn't nobody say you did that!" Indigo shot up out of the pillows, dragging Miranda with her to Mrs. Yancey's lap.

"That's not what I mean, sweetheart. Those be shooting words. I was suggesting that whoever be announcing that I grin up in the faces of these folks is out of they minds. All I do is go round the house that I be cleaning, waxing, dusting, ironing, sweeping . . . my regular chores. And if I come 'cross something that I gotta yen for, I say to the Mrs., 'I sho' do like that.' Then I stare at her, but with my eyes a lil bit going down and in a crooked direction. I look at what it was I wanted and look back at the white lady. I tell my soul to get all in what I want. Next thing you know the white lady can't think of no reason why she should have whatever that is. And she turn round asking me don't I want it, and of course I want it 'cause I done put all my soul in it. And I gotta have my soul in order to come on back round here to my house."

Indigo and Miranda thought about what Mrs. Yancey had said for days, but not nearly so much as they did about Mrs. Yancey and Mr. Henderson, also known as Uncle John the junk man. He was looking bad most of the time. Indigo figured that before she was born, Uncle John would have been called a fine looking man. Mrs. Yancey found no fault with that. Yet every time Uncle John would come round in his horse and wagon with things everybody didn't want, Mrs. Yancey would shudder, like the ugliness of whatall he carted startled her. She'd purse her lips, put her hands on her hips, whisper that cursing whisper Indigo had told Miranda about, or she would throw open her screen door and shout:

"John Henderson get that nasty mess out my face, get on away from my door with your trash, you hear me!"

Then she'd slam the door shut, brush her hands on her apron and pat her braids, as if she was making sure that nothing about her was as out of order as everything about Uncle John. Still, one day after she had shouted the daylights out the window for Uncle John to go on where ever it was that he laid his pitiful head, he came creeping up the steps.

Miranda and Indigo peeked out the window, being

careful to stay behind the curtains. Uncle John was a slight man, copper colored. Indigo explained to Miranda that that was the Indian in him. His eyes had a sly look, like the eyes of those boys that came tearing after Cypress after school; giggling eyes, and a mouth fitting a proud man. Mrs. Yancey looked more like Sister Mary Louise to Indigo. Here she was prancing around, twitching, putting her hair this way and that, because Uncle John was at the door. That didn't make no sense. No sense at all.

Uncle John had to push the bell three times. Finally, Mrs. Yancey slowly opened the wood door, leaving the screen door quite shut.

"Well, John Henderson, what are you doing on my front porch, looking how you look?"

She was right. Uncle John was a mite unkempt: white fuzzies curled from his ear, beneath his chin; his jacket was fraying at the lapels, and his shoes were covered with dirt. Mrs. Yancey hoped it was dirt, anyway. Uncle John, on the other hand, didn't pay no mind to Mrs. Yancey. He just looked at her with those giggling eyes and said:

"I been passing by here more frequent than I usedta, M'am. I'm not a young man no more, an' I been thinking how you collects nice things jus' like I do, an' how you still too smart looking to stay off by yourself all the time. I'm fixing to come calling in the nigh future if you don't mind?"

"John Henderson, you don't even have a place to live. You don't take baths, or shave. And you think you gonna grace my house with your I-don't-care-'bout-nothing-self. You don't even have a place to live."

"I'll just pass by round dinner time, awright." That's all he said, though he was grinning even as he patted his horse, Yoki. He must have been saying sweet things, because Yoki neighed, seemed to blush, and then they were gone.

Miranda had not said much about Mrs. Yancey and Uncle John, but Indigo figured that the way Mrs. Yancey carried on after he left that she set more store by him than she let on. That's why Indigo stole out of her mother's house quickly after their dinner of okra, rice and ham hocks, to see if Uncle John really came back, like he said he would. She carried Marie-Hélène with her, along with Miranda, because Marie-Hélène was so frail that she didn't get out much.

Indigo was really glad both her doll-friends were with her. Otherwise she would never have believed what she saw. Uncle John was there all right. Going up Mrs. Yancey's walk like he would have to, but he was in a tuxedo and top hat. The spats on his shoes gleamed in the lavender sky. He kept his pace up and his back straight with the help of an ebony cane with a gold handle. Plus, when Mrs. Yancey came to the door, her hair wasn't in braids. It was all over the place like those women in the pictures over bars, the mermaids covering their privates, with their hair flowing like seaweed everywhere. She wasn't wearing her slippers, either. She had on high heels and a pale blue dress chiseled onto her form like white on rice. Mrs. Yancey took Uncle John's arm; they virtually floated off the porch, down the walk to the corner.

Indigo kept hearing Mrs. Yancey say, "Uncle John you don't even have a place to live." Everybody knew Uncle John lived in his wagon, but nobody had ever seen what Indigo saw. Uncle John went over to his wagon, pulled out a fine easy chair and set it by the curb, then motioned for Mrs. Yancey to have a seat. Next thing Indigo knew, he had spread a Persian rug in the middle of the street, set a formal table, pulled out a wine bucket, and started dinner on the stove at the back of his wagon. Yoki was all dressed up with flowers woven through her mane and violet feathers tied on her hooves. Uncle John put candles on the table, and pinned a corsage to Mrs. Yancey's dress. She kept looking around like she thought being in the middle of the street in Uncle John's living room was not really safe, when out of nowhere the guys from the Geechee Capitans, a motorcycle gang of disrepute led by Pretty Man, came speeding down the street. Mrs. Yancey 'most jumped to her roof. Uncle John didn't exhibit much concern about these young ruffians on their huffing, humming bikes. He looked up, waved his hand, and the Geechee Capitans, who had never done a good turn by anybody in the city of Charleston, South Carolina, made road blocks on either side of Uncle John's parlor-in-the-middle-of-the-street.

Marie-Hélène told Indigo she thought she would faint. Miranda was speechless. Indigo tried to accept the Geechee Capitans, clad in leather jackets with crossed switchblades painted on their backs, pork-pie hats and black boots, guarding her friend Mrs. Yancey, who was having dinner with Uncle John the junk man in the street. Indigo stayed behind the bushes by the Johnsons' house as long as she could, looking. When Uncle John pulled out a Victrola, played a Fletcher Henderson 78, and asked Mrs. Yancey to dance, Indigo knew it was time to go home. There was too much magic out in the night. Indigo felt the moon in her mouth, singing. The South in her.

SUITORS WITH THE MOON'S BLESSING

Fill a glass that sparkles in sunlight with pure spring water. Place one sprig of fresh mint in the water, and a mouthful of honey. Take your middle finger gently round the curve of your lips as you imagine your beloved might. Kiss the edges of the finger. Take a breath so deep your groin senses it. Hold your breath while envisioning your beloved's face. Release the breath still picturing your beloved. Then with the kissed finger, make a circle round the rim of the glass 12 times, each time repeating your beloved's name. Each time seeing your beloved filled with joy. Close your eyes. Let your beloved fill your heart. Bring the glass to your lips. Drink the gladness that shall be yours.

IF YOUR BELOVED HAS EYES
FOR ANOTHER

Sleep on your left side with 6 white roses by your head. Fill your pillow with 2 handfuls of damiana leaves. Do this 3 days in a row. On the fourth day, use one handful of the damiana leaves to make tea. Drink 2 cups; one at dawn, the other at dusk. The other handful of damiana leaves should be mixed with cubeb berries, wrapped in a red or blue piece of cotton (use red if you have passions for your beloved. Use blue if you merely desire fidelity). With the damiana-cubeb berry-filled pouch anywhere on your person in the presence of your beloved, your way shall be had.

SEEKING NOTHING/
GIVING THANKS FOR LUNAR GIFTS
(Full moon required)

Bathe casually in a bath scented with cinnamon and vanilla. Wash hair with raspberry tea. Rinse thoroughly, being sure your hands have touched every part of your body as your beloved might. Without adornment of any kind, jewelry or clothing, go to the outside.

Lie fully open to the sky, widely, naked. Think of your beloved. Smell your beloved. Allow the Moon to share with you the pleasures your beloved brings you. Hold back nothing. Your thanks are mightily received. (May be executed in the company of your beloved, if he or she stands open over you, or if he or she lies as you lie at least 6 inches from you.) Before rising, you must have surrendered all you know of your beloved to the Moon, or your beloved shall have no more to offer you. (Very advanced. Wait if not sure.)

". . . 'And your sons will become shepherds in the wilderness.' Numbers 14:33. I think that's enough for you to meditate on tonight, Indigo."

"But that doesn't have anything to do with me, Sister Mary Louise!" Indigo squirmed in her seat where she was helping Sister Mary Louise select the flowers for the Little Shepherd of Judea, C.M.E. Church's Young People's Meeting.

"Don't blaspheme, Indigo. The Lord don't take kindly to senseless babblin'."

"I'm not babbling, Sister, really. I'm a girl, that's all. I want to know what I'm supposed to do." Indigo pushed the roses from this side to that, nimbly avoiding the thorns, handling buds with caring alacrity. This one will do. This one will not. Bruised flowers had no place on the altar in Christ's House. Sister Mary Louise was heartened when Indigo came round. Those other two, the one who went off to the North and the other one shaking her ass all the time, they had never learned how to touch flowers or the ways of the Lord. Sister Mary Louise with no children in her house invited Indigo, but

16/

not Indigo's doll friends, to be among her flowers, to join in singing the praises of the Lord Almighty whose blessings are so bountiful we can never give thanks enough, and to bake breads.

"You can take those loaves out the oven, and behave like a good Christian girl, that's what you can do."

Indigo looked at the roses and then at her friend, Mary Louise Murray, who must have been around roses too long. Her face shone like petals with veins glowing, like the opals she wore in her ears. One big plait lay smack in the middle of her head, wound round and round; serpents in the garden. Pale green eyes rushed from her face whenever the Holy Spirit took her, if her bushes were dewy and the sun just coming up. Indigo had a reluctant soul, to Sister Mary's mind. Not that Indigo was a bad child, only she'd been exposed to so many heathenish folks, pagans out there on those islands.

"Christian girls don't do nothing but bake bread?" Indigo peered into the oven. The heat beat her face till she frowned. "Not ready yet," she said, and carefully let the oven door fit back in its latch. Sister Mary Louise was tickled.

"No. Indigo, we don't just bake bread. We tend after beauty in the world. The flowers and the children." For all her Godfearing ways, Sister Mary Murray had been known to get the spirit outside of Church. Sometimes, when she was walking to the fish market or delivering breads, she'd be singing "I Ain't Got Weary Yet," or "Didn't My Lord Deliver Daniel," and she would just get happy in the street. This was not exemplary behavior for a Deaconess. At many a sermon she would be called forth to testify about how the Devil seized her in broad daylight, taking on the movements of the Holy Spirit, tempting the sinner in her. Other folks believed that being without children is what drove Sister Mary to have these fits in public. It only happened when some young boy from the country was within ten feet of her, broad shouldered and raw. Other folks figured that Sister Mary Louise sipped a little bit, and got to feeling so good she couldn't stand it. Indigo knew that Sister Mary Louise was in fact a Christian woman. Sister didn't allow any dolls that could talk in her house.

"No haints coming in my house. What do you imagine the Lord God Jesus Christ would think, if I set my table for haints?" That's what she'd said to Indigo.

Now Indigo was angry. The bread wasn't ready. Sister's saying little girls make bread and take care of beauty. Indigo thought her stomach was going to jump out of her mouth and knock over all the flowers, stomp the breads, and let hell aloose in Sister Mary's big white kitchen, where Jesus looked down from every wall. The Last Supper. The Annunciation. From way up on Mt. Calvary, there he was waiting for "his sons to shepherd." Indigo was so mad she felt lightheaded; hot all over.

"Sister Mary Louise, when I talked to Miranda she didn't want to bake nothing."

"I told you awready. You too big to be talking to dolls. Good Lord, Indigo, look at yourself." Indigo tried to focus on Sister Mary's face. But she only saw a glimmering. She tried to look at herself, and kept blinking her eyes, rubbing her palms over them, to get some focus. She saw something spreading out of her in a large scarlet pool at her feet. Sister Mary jumped up and down.

"Indigo the Lord's called you to be a woman. Look on High for His Blessing. Look I say. Look to Jesus, who has 'blessed you this day.' " Indigo fell down on her knees like Sister Mary had. And listened and swayed in her growing scarlet lake to the voice of this green-eyed woman singing for the heavens: "Trouble In Mind," "Done Made My Vow," and "Rise and Shine," so that Indigo would know "among whom was Mary Magdalene."

"Speak, child, raise your voice that the Lord May Know You as the Woman You Are."

Then Sister Mary Louise rose, her thin body coated with Indigo's blood. She gently took off Indigo's clothes, dropped them in a pail of cold water. She bathed Indigo in a hot tub filled with rose petals: white, red, and yellow floating around a new woman. She made Indigo a garland of flowers, and motioned for her to go into the back yard.

"There in the garden, among God's other beauties, you should spend these first hours. Eve's curse threw us out the garden. But like I told you, women tend to beauty and children. Now you can do both. Take your blessing and let your blood flow among the roses. Squat like you will when you give birth. Smile like you will when God chooses to give you a woman's pleasure. Go now, like I say. Be not afraid of your nakedness."

Then Sister Mary shut the back door. Indigo sat bleeding among the roses, fragrant and filled with grace.

MARVELOUS MENSTRUATING MOMENTS *(As Told by Indigo to Her Dolls as She Made Each and Every One of Them a Personal Menstruation Pad of Velvet)*

A. *Flowing:*

When you first realize your blood has come, smile; an honest smile, for you are about to have an intense union with your magic. This is a private time, a special time, for thinking and dreaming. Change your bedsheet to the

19/

ones that are your favorite. Sleep with a laurel leaf under your head. Take baths in wild hyssop, white water lilies. Listen for the voices of your visions; they are nearby. Let annoying people, draining worries, fall away as your body lets what she doesn't need go from her. Remember that you are a river; your banks are red honey where the Moon wanders.

B. *For Disturbance of the Flow:*

Don't be angry with your body if she is not letting go of her blood. Eat strawberries, make strawberry tea with the leaves to facilitate the flow. To increase the flow, drink squaw weed tea. For soothing before your blood flows, drink some black snakeroot or valerian tea. For cramps, chew wild ginger.

"Indigo, I don't want to hear another word about it, do you understand me. I'm not setting the table with my Sunday china for fifteen dolls who got their period today!"

"But, Mama, I promised everybody we'd have a party because we were growing up and could be more like women. That's what Sister Mary Louise said. She said that we should feast and celebrate with our very best dresses and our very favorite foods."

"Sister Mary Louise needs to get herself married 'fore she's lost what little of her mind she's got left. I don't want you going round that simple woman's house. You take my good velvet from 'tween those dolls' legs. Go to the store and buy yourself some Kotex. Then you come back here and pack those creatures up. Put them in the attic. Bring yourself back here and I'm going to tell you the truth of what you should be worrying about now you sucha grown woman."

"Mama, I can't do that. I can't put them away. I'll have nobody to talk to. Nobody at all."

"Indigo, you're too big for this nonsense. Do like I say, now."

"Mama. What if I stopped carrying Miranda in the street with me, and left my other friends upstairs all the time, could I leave 'em out then, could I? Please Mama, I know they're dollies. I really do. Sassafrass and Cypress kept all the things they made when they were little, didn't they?"

"That's a lie. Don't you have all their dolls? I can't believe a girl as big as you, wearing a training bra and stockings to school, can't think of nothing but make-believe. But if you promise me that you going to leave them in your room and stop asking me to sing to 'em, feed 'em, and talk with 'em, you can leave them out. Now go on to the store."

Indigo left her lesson book on the kitchen table, went to her mother tearing collards by the sink, and gave her a big hug. Her mother's apron always smelled like cinnamon and garlic no matter how many times it was washed. It smelled of times like this when her mother felt a surge in her bosom like her nipples were exploding with milk again, leaving her damp and sweet, but now it was Indigo's tears that softened her spirit.

"Indigo, you're my littlest baby, but you make it hard for me sometimes, you know that."

"Mama, I can make it easier today 'cause I aweady know what it is you were gonna tell me when I came back from the store."

"You do, do you?"

"Yeah, you were going to tell me that since I became a woman, boys were gonna come round more often, 'cause they could follow the trail of stars that fall from between my legs after dark."

"What?"

"The stars that fall from 'tween my legs can only be seen by boys who are pure of mind and strong of body."

"Indigo, listen to me very seriously. This is Charleston, South Carolina. Stars don't fall from little colored girls' legs. Little boys don't come chasing after you for nothing good. White men roam these parts with evil in their blood, and every single thought they have about a colored woman is dangerous. You have gotta stop living this make-believe. Please, do that for your mother."

"Every time I tell you something, you tell me about white folks. 'White folks say you can't go here—white folks say you can't do this—you can't do that.' I didn't make up white folks, what they got to do with me? I ain't white. My dolls ain't white. I don't go round bothering white folks!"

"That's right, they come round bothering us, that's what I'm trying to tell you . . ."

"Well if they bothering you so much, you do something about 'em."

"Is that some sass comin' out your mouth?"

"No, M'am. It's just I don't understand why any ol' white person from outta nowhere would want to hurt us. That's all."

Indigo moved to her mother, with a seriousness about her that left the kitchen emptied of all its fullness and aroma.

"I love you so much, Mama. & you are a grown colored woman. Some white man could just come hurt you, any time he wants, too? Oh I could just kill 'em, if they hurt you, Mama. I would. I would just kill anybody who hurt you."

Holding her child as tight as she could, as close into herself as she could, the mother whispered as softly as she could, as lovingly as she could: "Well, then we'll both be careful & look after each. Won't we?"

Indigo sort of nodded her head, but all she remembered was that even her mother was scared of white folks, and that she still wrote out the word Kotex on a piece of torn paper wrapped up in a dollar bill to give to Mr. Lucas round to the pharmacy. This, though Indigo insisted Mr. Lucas must know what it is, 'cause he ordered it for his store so all the other colored women could have it when they needed it. After all, even her mother said, this bleeding comes without fail to every good girl once a month. Sometimes her mother made no sense at all, Indigo thought with great consternation. On the other hand, as a gesture of goodwill & in hopes that her littlest girl would heed her warnings, the mother allowed Indigo one more public jaunt with Miranda, who was, according to Indigo, fraught with grief that their outings were to be curtailed.

Weeping willows curled up from the earth, reaching over Indigo & Miranda on this their last walk in a long friendship, a simple, laughing friendship. Miranda thought the weeping willows were trying to hug them, to pull them up to the skies where whether you were real or not didn't matter. Indigo, in her most grown-up voice, said, "No, they want us to feel real special on this day, that's all." Miranda wasn't convinced, and neither was Indigo, who managed to take the longest walk to the drugstore that her family had ever known.

After following the willows' trellises till there were no more, Indigo reverently passed by Mrs. Yancey's, back round to Sister Mary Louise's, down to the wharf where she & Miranda waved to her father who was living in the sea with mermaids, & then 'cross to the railroad tracks looking for Uncle John. Indigo liked colored folks who worked with things that took 'em some place: colored folks on ships, trains, trolleys, & horses. Yoki was a horse. Uncle John did go places, and after that night with Mrs. Yancey in the street, Indigo figured him mighty powerful.

In between two lone railroad cars was Uncle John's wagon. Sequestered from ill-wishers & the wind, there he was chatting away with the air, the cars, or Yoki. Sometimes men of Color disappear into the beauty of the light, especially toward day's end. It's like clouds take on color & get down on the ground & talk to you, or the stars jump in some black man's body & shine all over you. Uncle John was looking like that to Indigo's mind, just brushing away, leaving Yoki's coat glimmering like dusk.

"Good evening, Uncle John."

"Humph." Mr. Henderson turned round knowing full well who'd come calling, but not wanting to let on. "Oh. If it ain't my girl Indigo. & who's that ya got witcha?"

"This is Miranda. We're going to Mr. Lucas' to pick up something." Indigo was quite careful not to say what she was going to the drugstore for, 'cause her mother had said not to say anything to anybody.

"Indigo, Mr. Lucas' place way off from heah, don't ya think?"

"Well, Uncle John, that's some of it, but not all of it."

Laying down his brush, pulling a stool from the other side of a fire where he was cooking either a chicken or a pigeon, Uncle John motioned for Indigo to take a seat.

"Some of it, but t'aint all of it, ya say? Well, I would be guessin' the rest of it be a matter for discussion."

"Yes, Uncle John. I want you to tell me something.

I'm asking you 'cause you been doin' what suits your
own mind since I was born."

"No, long fo' that, chile."

"Well, anyway, I want to keep on talkin' with all my
dolls. You know they my very best friends." Indigo was
talking so fast now, Uncle John started walking in a
circle around her so as to understand better. " & Mama
wants me to put 'em way 'cause now I am a woman &
who will I talk to? I can't seem to get on with the chirren
in the school I go ta. I don't like real folks near as
much." Indigo had jumped off the stool with Miranda in
her arms, much like a woman daring someone to touch
her child. Uncle John stood still for a minute, looking
at the shadows of the rail cars on Yoki's back.

"Indigo, times catch up on everybody. Me & Yoki
heah been catched up by trains & grocery stores. Now
you bein' catched up by ya growin' up. That's what ya
mama's tryin' to say to ya. Ya gotta try to be mo' in this
world. I know, it don't suit me either."

Miranda was crying, nestled in Indigo's elbow. Uncle
John mumbled to himself, & climbed in his wagon. Indigo stayed put. Folks said that sometimes, when Uncle
John had said all he had to say, he got in his wagon &
that was that. Other times folks said Uncle John would
get in his wagon & come back out with something to keep
your life moving along sweeter. So Indigo didn't move
a muscle. Miranda prayed some good would come of all
this. They still hadn't gone to Mr. Lucas'. Indigo could
hear Uncle John humming to himself, fumbling in that
wagon. He was looking for something for her so she
could keep talkin' & not have to be with them real folks
& all their evil complicated ways of doing. The last of the
day's sun settled on Indigo's back, warmed the taut
worry out of her limbs, & sat her back down on the stool,
jabbering away to Miranda.

25/

"See, you thought that I was gonna just go on & do
what Mama said & never play witya no more or go
explore & make believe. See, see, ya didn't have no
faith. What's that Sister Mary Louise is all the time
sayin'?"

"Oh ye of lil faith . . ." Miranda rejoined.

Uncle John didn't come out of his wagon first. A fiddle
did. Uncle John was holding it, of course, but he poked
the fiddle out, then one leg, his backside, and the other
leg, his precious greying head, and the last arm with a
bow in his grasp. Indigo & Miranda were suspicious.

"What we need a violin for?" Miranda sniggled.

"Hush, Miranda, Uncle John knows what he's doin'.
Just wait a minute, will ya?"

Uncle John sure nuf had intentions to give this fiddle
to Indigo. His face was beaming, arms wide open, with
the fiddle & bow tracing the horizons, moving toward
Indigo who was smiling with no reason why.

"Indigo, this heah is yo' new talkin' friend."

"A fiddle, Uncle John?" Indigo tried to hide her
disappointment, but Miranda hit her in her stomach.
"Uh, that's not what I need, Uncle John." She sat back
on the stool like she'd lost her backbone. Uncle John was
a bit taken back, but not swayed.

"Listen now, girl. I'ma tell ya some matters of the
reality of the unreal. In times blacker than these," Uncle
John waved the violin & the bow toward the deepening
night, "when them slaves was ourselves & we couldn't
talk free, or walk free, who ya think be doin' our talkin'
for us?"

"White folks, of course," snapped Indigo.

Uncle John's face drew up on his bones like a small
furious fire. His back shot up from his legs like a mahog-
any log.

"Whatchu say, gal?? I caint believe ya tol' me some

white folks was doin' our talkin'. Now, if ya want me to help ya, don't say nary another word to me till I'm tellin' ya I'm finished. Now, listen. Them whites what owned slaves took everythin' was ourselves & didn't even keep it fo' they own selves. Just threw it on away, ya heah. Took them drums what they could, but they couldn't take our feet. Took them languages what we speak. Took off wit our spirits & left us wit they Son. But the fiddle was the talkin' one. The fiddle be callin' our gods what left us/be givin' back some devilment & hope in our bodies worn down & lonely over these fields & kitchens. Why white folks so dumb, they was thinkin' that if we didn't have nothin' of our own, they could come controllin', meddlin', whippin' our sense on outta us. But the Colored smart, ya see. The Colored got some wits to em, you & me, we ain't the onliest ones be talkin' wit the unreal. What ya think music is, whatchu think the blues be, & them get happy church musics is about, but talkin' wit the unreal what's mo' real than most folks ever gonna know."

With that Uncle John placed the fiddle in the middle of his left arm & began to make some conversations with Miranda & Indigo. Yes, conversations. Talkin' to em. Movin' to an understandin' of other worlds. Puttin' the rhythm in a good sit down & visit. Bringin' the light out a good cry. Chasing the night back round yonder. Uncle John pulled that bow, he bounced that bow, let the bow flirt with those strings till both Miranda & Indigo were most talkin' in tongues. Like the slaves who were ourselves had so much to say, they all went on at once in the voices of the children: this child, Indigo.

When Indigo first tried to hold the fiddle under her neck like the children in the orchestra at school, Uncle John just chuckled, looked away. When she had it placed nearer her armpit & closer to her heart, with the

bow tucked indelicately in her palm, he said, "Now talk
to us, girl." Indigo hesitated, pulled the bow toward the
A string, took a breath, & stopped. "I don't know how
to play a violin, Uncle John."

"Yeah, ya do. Tell Miranda somethin' on that fiddle.
'Cause after today, ya won't be able to reach out to her
like ya do now. Ya gonna haveta call her out, wit that
fiddle."

Indigo looked at Miranda lying on the stool & then
back at Uncle John whose eyes were all over her face,
the fiddle, the bow. & in a moment like a fever, Indigo
carried that bow cross those fiddle strings till Miranda
knew how much her friend loved her, till the slaves who
were ourselves made a chorus round the fire, till Indigo
was satisfied she wasn't silenced. She had many tongues,
many spirits who loved her, real & unreal.

The South in her.

It was already so late Mr. Lucas had started to lock
up his shop. Only the lights in the very back were still
on. Indigo held onto her violin with its musty case reli-
giously, & she beat on the doors of the pharmacy like
somebody possessed. "Please open up, Mr. Lucas. It's
a emergency," she shouted. Mr. Lucas, portly & honey
brown, peered out the door thru the lettering: Lucas'
Pharmacy, Oldest Negro Drugstore in Charleston, S.C.
Between the "S" & the "C" there was Indigo's face,
churning & shouting. Mr. Lucas opened up remarking,
"An emergency is somebody dyin' or a woman who
needs some Kotex." Indigo was stunned. "Hi, Mr.
Lucas, how'd you know that?"

"Oh, I been in this business a long time, Indigo. Tell
your mother she almost missed me this time."

"Oh, it's not for Mama, it's for me." All of a sudden
Indigo blushed & shrank. She'd gone & done what her
mother had asked her please not to do. Mr. Lucas took

a step toward Indigo, like he was looking for the woman in her. He'd seen younger girls than Indigo who were busy having babies. He'd even seen girls more comely in a grown-woman manner than she who didn't bleed at all. But here was this girl with this child body & woman in her all at once. It was difficult for Mr. Lucas to just go & get the Kotex. He wanted to keep looking at this girl, this woman. He wanted to know what she felt like.

Indigo heard somebody talking to her. She saw Mr. Lucas coming toward her & somebody talking to her. Telling her to get the Kotex & get home quick. Get the Kotex & get home quick. Indigo ran to the back of the store, grabbed the blue box, stuffed it under her arm with Miranda & whipped thru the aisles with Mr. Lucas behind her, lumbering, quiet. The fiddle was knocking all kinds of personal hygiene products off shelves: tooth-paste, deodorant, shaving cream. Indigo almost dropped it, but she held tighter, moved faster, heard somebody telling her to get home quick. She got to the doors, started to look back & didn't. She just opened the door as best she could without letting go of anything & ran out.

Mr. Lucas stood in the back of his pharmacy, looking at his S.C. Certification, his diploma from Atlanta University. He knew he might be in some trouble. Didn't know what had got hold to him. Every once in a while, he saw a woman with something he wanted. Something she shouldn't have. He didn't know what it was, an irreverence, an insolence, like the bitch thought she owned the moon.

"Yeah, that's right." Mr. Lucas relaxed. "The whole town knows that child's crazed. If she says a thing, won't a soul put no store in it."

The South in her.

29/

Ntozake Shange

TO RID ONESELF OF THE SCENT
OF EVIL*
by Indigo

(Traditional Method)
Though it may cause some emotional disruptions, stand absolutely still & repeat the offender's name till you are overwhelmed with the memory of your encounter. Take two deep slow breaths, on a 7 count. Then, waving your arms & hands all about you, so your atmosphere may again be clean, say the name of the offender softly. Each time blowing your own breath into the world that we may all benefit from your renewal. Then in a hot place (your kitchen or out of doors) cover yourself in warm clay poultices. Let them dry on you, taking the poisons of the offender out of your body & spirit. Run a steaming shower over your body, allowing all grime & other to fall from you without using your hands or a cloth. Then, run yourself a new tub full of warm water filled with angelica & chamomile. Bring to your bath a tall clear glass of spring water wherein floats one closed white rose. Lying in your fragrant bath, sip the rose's water, for you are again among nature's flowers.

(For Modern Times)
Drink a strong mix of lemon tea & honey. This, if you've not cheated, should bring sweat to your brow. This is the poison the offender has left lurking. As you sweat, draw a bath that sends steam up toward your face, if you are

*(Violence or purposeful revenge should not be considered in most cases. Only during wars of national liberation, to restore the honor of the race, or to redress calamitous personal & familial trauma, may we consider brute force/annihilation.)

30/

on your knees. Take a piece of silk or cotton to which you feel attached & that bodes of happier times. Fill it with caraway seeds. Tie it with a ribbon that is your oldest female relative's favorite color. Float it in your bath. Stand naked over your tub. Kiss your right shoulder. Then your left. Step breathing briskly into the water. You shall be cleaned of all the offender's toxic presence.

*I*ndigo did not tell her mother about Mr. Lucas being so evil, nor did she mention that her new fiddle could talk. These notions would bring her mother's ire up & out. Nowadays Indigo minded what she said & to whom. Some folks you tell some things, some folks you don't. With the dolls all lined up in her room now, no longer going calling, coming down for dinner, Indigo kept her window open all the time. She told her mother this was just for health reasons. Why New England people sleep with the windows open in snow: gives the body & spirit strength. Now, her mother didn't want her own windows open, but it seemed like Indigo was making more reasonable connections. The windows in the child's room stayed open.

Indigo invited the Moon in to sing to her doll-companions, mute though they were. She thought they had trouble sleeping. When the night air danced about them, leaving the shivers of that embrace, Indigo would take out her violin & play the way she learned. Letting the instrument speak right up. Giving another space to all the feelings her little girl's body could not always contain. The talking music aroused the dolls to celebrate.

Indigo sat in her window, working with her fiddle, telling everybody, the wind & all his brothers, what was on her mind, the turmoil in the spirit realm, the luxuriant realities she meandered in her sleep. Whenever she wanted to pray, she let her fiddle talk. Whenever she was angry, here came the fiddle. All the different ways of handling a violin & bow came to Indigo as she needed. They came: *legato, staccato, andante, forte, fortissimo, piano, allegro, presto.*

"Indigo, we're going to have to talk about this violin." Indigo was startled by her mother's nocturnal visit. The breeze felt good on her face. Indigo turned gently from the soft rumble of a sea-town night to her mother.

"Oh, I'm so glad, Mama. I wanted to talk to you about the fiddle some more, but I was afraid you . . ."

"Why Indigo, how could you think I wouldn't find somebody to give you lessons. I gave Sassafrass every weaving lesson she asked for, sent Cypress to New York for her dancing. Why wouldn't I give you violin lessons? Surely, there's one brave soul in Charleston who'll take this terrible-playing child of mine."

Indigo looked at her mother for a long while. Her mother feeling very proud of her daughter who'd tried to teach herself how to play the fiddle, who'd given up talking out of her head, talking only to her dolls. She glanced at her child's handiwork, Marie-Hélène, Miranda, Susie-Q, Candace, Lilli, fingering their hats and petticoats delicately. Now Indigo was involved with music which she would be as diligent & loving about as she had about her dolls, her companions, as she called them. The mother looked over to Indigo still sitting in the window. Not a word did she say, there in the window with her violin in an acceptable rest position.

"Now Indigo, what do you say to real violin lessons

& closing that window so our neighbors can be spared this racket till you've learned a bit more?" Approaching her daughter with some glee, the mother stopped when Indigo turned her back, stood up, & began making those strange, erratic, annoying non-songs she played each night, that Miz Fitzhugh had complained about twice, along with the Daltons. Even Mr. Epps who lived three doors down & across the street had stopped by on his way to the post office to say, "Please do something about those noises from your house, or I'll have to call the constable round this way."

No, Indigo would not have her way this time. She wasn't going to be run out of her own home cause Indigo was playing a violin. She had to have some lessons 'cause these folks didn't realize the passion her daughter had for the violin.

"Indigo, I promise you. I'll get you the best teacher I can find." Indigo stopped slowly, C#, fifth position, D string.

"Mama, I'm happy with how the fiddle's talk . . . sounding now. I don't want any lessons at all. I just want to play." Thinking her mother was relieved, Indigo left the window. She put the violin away, even closed the gingham curtains. Indigo smiled up at her mama, who had a most curious expression. No matter what she did, Indigo was always beyond her reason. A good girl, yet out of reach.

"Mama, what's wrong? I said you don't have to get me lessons. I'm just fine."

"Indigo, you may have those lessons whenever you like & I mean that. But until you decide to take them, I can't allow you to make that noise in my house. I've got enough trouble on my hands without having every neighbor I've got thinking we got banshees living in here at night. Besides, Miz Fitzhugh, herself, even mentioned to me how unpleasant your violin-playing actually is, right now. I don't mean to say you won't be a wonderful musician in the future. But, Indigo, you may not submit the whole world to your will. No lessons, no violin playing under this roof."

Indigo sat back on her bed 'tween Candace & Marie-Hélène, who whispered: "Listen, I've gotta idea, Indigo."

"Mama, would you be mad if I played it someplace else? Outside, somewhere?"

Imagining she could use a nice hot toddy, the mother was going out Indigo's door, when she turned round to say that Indigo could take the violin anywhere out of the neighborhood & make any noise she liked 'cause then she would have to talk to the strangers beseeching her: "Please, get a lesson, girl," which is precisely what her mother had said.

Indigo patted the violin by her bed exactly where Aunt Haydee kept her shotgun. "No, Mama, that's not what's gonna happen." She kissed Miranda good-night & went to sleep. Her mother left a glass of cider & a deep chocolate on Indigo's night stand. It was midnight & the Moon was full.

Sister Mary Louise put Indigo & her violin behind the shed where she kept her gardening tools—shovels, vitamins for roses & violets, peat moss, watering cans, heavy gloves, rakes, & strings. Too much of the Holy Ghost came out of Indigo & that fiddle. Sister Mary Louise swore even she couldn't stand that much spirit every day. "Back there behind the shed, Indigo, is just fine. Come anytime ya like. If I feel callt, I'ma come on out & listen." That's what Sister Mary Louise had decided about that. "Good for the plants. Too much order, too much gentility'll make my flowers more prim than glorious. We all need a lil wildness." So here came Indigo every day after school plying her new medium out back.

Indigo wanted to sound like the sparrows & wrens. She mimicked the jays & peckers. Conversing with gulls was easy 'cause they saw her daddy's soul every day. Indigo had mastered the hum of dusk, the crescendoes of the cicadas, swamp rushes in light winds, thunder at high tide, & her mother's laughter down the hall. Uncle John told her one time when they were frying porgies by his wagon that he'd got this feeling in his waking up that Indigo was dwelling dangerous on the misery of the slaves who were ourselves, & this feeling directed him to march her toward the beauty of this world & the joys of the those come before us. Indigo couldn't get enough. No creature that moved escaped Indigo's attention. If the fiddle talked, it also rumbled, cawed, rustled, screamed, sighed, sirened, giggled, stomped, & sneered. Every once in a while Indigo even played songs. Some colored singing, Tina Turner, B. B. King, Etta James: they songs. This was a secret. Indigo had some pride & couldn't admit to those who claimed she made noise all the time that she'd found out the difference 'tween her free communion with the universe, primal, unrelenting flights, & melody. She played these softly, for herself. Then she'd blush, hurriedly put the fiddle back into the case, the Colored & Romance having got the best of her. Young boys were alien to her. She didn't want to be a fool in love, have something terrible getta holdt to her. When she'd had enough of "sweetheart," "babeee," & "please, please, please," Indigo yelped, "Oh Sister Mary Louise, you missed that."

There was something moving up her leg, something that was not supposed to be there. Indigo looked down, lost a little fear, just a twig. How was a twig going up

& down the inside of her leg, tickling her like the "sweet-hearts" & "babees" she'd been playing. Indigo looked cautiously behind her where two brown-skinned boys leaned over Sister Mary Louise's fence.

"Get that twig from 'tween my legs."

"We just tryin' to get ya attention. Ya so busy fiddlin' ya don't see nobody. Where ya learn to play like that, gal?"

"My name ain't 'gal' & I taught myself. Now go on 'way & leave me be, please." Indigo hoped they hadn't heard her playing songs, but her wild sounds. She hadda hunch it was them Romance riffs that brought these fellas by the shed. Nobody ever came behind Sister Mary Louise's house. There were devils, Mandingo giants, quadroon elves, & wayward ghosts in her shed.

"What's your name, sweetheart?" the taller boy asked. This one in worn jeans particularly frayed at the edges the way the Geechee Capitans wore theirs when they went crabbing. His head was shaved to keep from the ringworm, Indigo surmised. But the boy had such a pretty head. It was not flat in the back, a pancake head, nor was it all forced up above his eyes, a waterhead. No, this boy had a pretty nutmeg head. He was still slipping that stick round Indigo's ankle though, & she'd told him to stop. The other boy was real stocky, a flathead, but high cheekbones. Indigo recognized the blood of that colored family married Chinese. They all looked like that. Still there was no doubt she'd told them to leave her be & they didn't. Indigo closed her eyes tight like she was fixing to run or scream; instead she said: *"Falcon come in this fiddle. Falcon come in this fiddle. Leopard come in this fiddle. Leopard come in this fiddle. I'm on the prey. I'm on the prey."* 'Fore she knew it, Indigo was so busy bowing the daylights & jungles out her violin, she didn't notice the two boys duck down on the other side of the fence. When she opened her eyes, she realized she'd stood her ground. & that stick was no longer 'tween her legs. She smiled a tiny smile, peered over the fence, tapped the tall boy's shin with the tip of the bow.

"What's your name, sweetheart?" Indigo chirped, so fulla herself. The boys brushed the sand from their knees, grinned self-consciously.

"I'm Spats," the tall boy answered, "& this here is Crunch. We Junior Geechee Capitans."

Indigo held her tongue. "Why imagine that. Y'all Junior G.C. Ain't that somethin'. I'm Indigo."

Spats jumped over the fence first. He reached for Indigo's fiddle. She pulled it away gracefully. "I can't let anyone touch my instrument. It's bad luck." Spats shrugged his shoulders. "Hey, whatever ya say. Ain't that right, Crunch?" Crunch hanging tough in the alleyway was hardly enthusiastic. A girl with a violin had got him down on his knees in broad daylight.

"What the hell was ya doin' on that damn thing?" Crunch grumbled, messing with his elbows, his thick crop of black hair meeting his furrowed indignant brow.

"I was fightin' back in my own way. That's what I was doin'. & you know it. Come puttin' a stick 'tween my legs like I ain't got no better sense than to let you do it 'cause you boys. Um-humph. Uncle John, he spoke to me on that. He said, 'Indigo, when trouble come, get your fiddle.' "

Spats & Crunch stared at each other. How could a girl know Uncle John? What was Uncle John doing giving some girl all his advice & counsel? Why their seniors, the real Geechee Capitans, held counsel with Uncle John. Very impressed, a little riled, the two boys folded their arms cross their chests & began a culturally recognized & universally feared ritual: The Geechee Capitan

Cock Walk. Spats took off his sweatshirt with no sleeves, a slit down the middle, turned inside-out anyway, threw it on the ground. Crunch peeled his black tee-shirt from his ample torso, threw it on the ground. They clapped their hands. Clap. Clapclap. Clap. Spit on the ground, once to the east & once to the west. Then they walked in a circle round Indigo. Slow-n-don't-mess-round clock-wise. Slow-n-this-might-be-the-last-time counter clock-wise. Again. Humph. Again. Humph. Clap. Clapclap. Clap.

Indigo'd been round long enough to know that she was either being initiated or 'bout to die. Crunch was not too excited 'bout the powers of her fiddlin'. Spats was probably more physical than his slight frame intimated. Indigo held her breath. Next thing was gonna happen, was somebody'd break the rhythm & whoever that was had better be on the case or die.

Spats moved first, fast. Had Indigo on his small shoul-ders 'fore Crunch could move all of himself anywhere. There was still the possibility that Crunch might plow into them or belly-whip 'em to a tumble. Spats glanced up at Indigo, who was delighted to be such a prize & safe. Crunch kept his flat face straight: "Awright man, she in." Indigo jumped offa Spats, jubilant. The real world was workin' its way up. Crunch didn't like that she was a girl, but whoever could scare a G.C., even the Jr. G.C.'s, had the right to be initiated or die. Plus, a some-body who was already a G.C. hadta put his honor on the line: to really save the person from all the rest, or do harm to the person in the face of all the other G.C.'s. Now it was also true there were only two members of the Jr. Geechee Capitans, Spats & Crunch. That's 'cause they hadn't met anybody could fight as well as they could. Till Indigo. Crunch really didn't like that she was a girl. Spats liked that.

39/

Indigo had a moon in her mouth after all. With Spats & Crunch to run with, her workings, as she called them, were more down to earth. Indigo's specialities were other worlds, fiddling. Spats concentrated on hands, deft, light knife throwing-get-a-watch-offa-wrist, agile hands. Crunch, himself, was moved by yearnings to tear-the-damn-place-down, your place, you, anybody he hadda hankering to. Awesome trio. The immediate problem was how to identify Indigo as a Jr. G.C. Spats almost slapped the devil out of Crunch when he said, "Man, that's impossible. She a girl, how she gonna look like us?" Spats snarled, "Ain't nothin' impossible for a Gee-chee Cap-i-tan." With that the two assembled Indigo's uniform. 'Cause she wouldn't look right in a inside-out sweatshirt or in cut-offs like theirs, they decided on a hat. Spats stole a Stetson, the smallest one he saw in Kerreson's. They didn't like the Colored to try the hats on anyway. Crunch beat up some yellow hincty boy who was playing ball on King Street & took a fine leather belt off him. Then they decorated it with switchblade handles & a strap for Indigo to carry her fiddle round. What Geechee Capitan would walk round without having both hands free? In her new get-up Indigo was a fierce-looking lil sister. She stuffed her braids up in her Stetson, dark brown & tilted over her left eye. Spats, Crunch, & Indigo, all agreed that she was now presentable. Nevertheless, Crunch felt something was missing.

"Hey, Spats, I know what's wrong! She ain't gotta real name. Ya know, a name particular to us!" Indigo had always liked her name. There was nothing wrong with her name. She was particularly herself. She changed the nature of things. She colored & made richer what was blank & plain. The slaves who were ourselves knew all about indigo & Indigo herself. Besides there was great danger in callin' someone out their name. Spirits get confused, bring you something meant for someone else. Folks get upset, move with wrath instead of grace, when callt by a name not blessed & known on earth. Indigo was not hot on this new name business. After some discussion, Crunch accepted a shortening of Indigo to "Digo." Spats had learned enough to know that in another language, Spanish to be exact, "digo" had something to do with "to say" & to his mind, Digo was really sayin' somethin'. If she chose to get on her fiddle, ya best mind what she say.

The South in her.

Coming down Chad Street or running thru the Yards, the Jr. G.C.'s served notice that the colored children were manifestations of the twentieth century. No mythology in the Old Slave Mart approached their realities. Nothing in the Calhoun House reminded them of themselves. Catfish Row was so old-fashioned, dusted pastel frame houses where hominy-grits, oysters, & okra steamed each evening. Crap games went on as usual in the tiny alleyways, edged by worn porches where grandmas made believe they didn't have any idea all that was goin' on. Yet they'd smile if somebody had a high streak of luck, sending yelps & bass guffaws over the roofs. Here Digo, Crunch, & Spats performed, mixing the skills of modern wayward children with the past-times of the more traditional colored iconoclasts.

They especially liked to go round to Sneed's. Now, Sneed's was a bakery; fresh breads, muffins, cakes, & cookies every day. But the reasons the Jr. G.C.'s spent so much time there was that Sneed's was connected to a winding complex of underground rooms where gambling, cockfights, and a twenty-four-hour social room entertained the most adventurous of Charleston's colored subterraneans. Spats' brother, Pretty Man, made sure that the transactions in the various gaming activities stayed calm. Whenever possible, Pretty Man believed that money should change hands in his favor, calmly, of course.

Actually, the bakers in their high white hats & flour-covered aprons carried more than dough downstairs directly under the ovens. They took the daily numbers receipts down to The Caverns, as they were called, & came back up to the muffins & turnovers with a possible change of life-style for a confirmed pastry-gourmet. Indigo didn't mind the numbers. She played a few from time to time. That meant new dress-up clothes, Eudoxa strings for the violin, a Sunday chapeau for Mama, and spending change for the spirits who still kept Indigo's company late at night.

NUMBERS FOR PROSPERITY &
FURTHERED INDEPENDENCE
OF THE RACE
by Indigo

164—if searching for hearth & home, more secure familial relations.

626—if desirous of a journey to one's true home, spiritual or physical, play once a week for a month.

208—if in need of immediate assistance for ordinary amenities, play only on Monday.

176—if seeking a larger dwelling for one's family, this works, in conjunction with 164.

508—if yearning for retreat & personal solitude, play on five consecutive Wednesdays.

141—*if conflicted by the stresses of racism, play twice a week for five years.*
999—*to be freed from debilitating relations, fiscal or otherwise, daily.*

REALIZING SPIRITS' HINTS /
WHAT YOUR DREAMS CAN DO FOR YOU
by Indigo

If you see a gull flying over your house, there is a 7 in your combination. If the gull swoops downward, there is also a 2. If the gull flies toward the moon, there is a 9.

If your Mother is burning something on the stove, and you cannot get up to warn her, play 1. If she is burning up something, and you are able to warn her, play 7. If what your Mother is cooking & burning is your favorite dish, that's a 123, in combination.

If there is a lover of yours kissing your best friend in your house, there are two 3's in your number. If you are angry about this, your number is 353. If you find it amusing, your number is 333.

If you keep falling down in your dream, there's surely an 8 in your number. If where you are falling is never reached or is unknown, add a 1. If you fall somewhere, change that to 6.

GENERAL NOTES

Flowers—719/ A car—520/ Fires—882/ Beds— 231/ The Christ Child—777/ The Crucifix—111/ Judas (someone you know or Iscariot)—001/ A deceased

43/

grandmother—803/ A deceased grandfather—902/
Mulberry bushes—756/ Maggots—395/ Guns—246.

Pretty Man hired Spats & Crunch to clean up after the cockfights. To carry the screeching bleeding birds on outside & kill 'em, if need be, was Spats' job. Taking the razors off their feet was Crunch's. Indigo stayed away from the ring after the first time. She'd watched these men shouting out for their favorite to slay the other. All this money waving in their hands, collected by Pretty Man, who must have been a mathematical genius. He kept all the odds, paid out, collected what was due him, without taking his eyes off the match. Indigo felt a steely vengeance growing in her spirit. Grown men laughing at dying animals. She felt birds hovering above her eyes. She moved the razors off the roosters. Put them in the palms of the onlookers. Let them cut each other to shreds, she thought. Let them know the havoc of pain. Spats & Crunch had suspicions 'bout Indigo's powers, but couldn't believe she'd gone & done something like this.

The cocks stalked the ring quietly. The men round the ring leaped over one another, flailing their razored palms at throats, up & down backs, backsides, ankles. Such a conglomeration of footwear swung over the side of the ring: high-top sneakers, lizard loafers, wing-tips, galoshes, work boots. Indigo stood by the door watching this bloodletting. Silent. Pretty Man surveyed the situation. Put the evilest eye he could gather up on Indigo, who startled under the power of his gaze. That was all it took. The men slowly came back to themselves. Looked about, puzzled. Put their hats back on. Shook the sawdust from themselves. Wondered where all this blood in the stands came from. The wounds had closed, no scars. Indigo was not malevolent. Yet Pretty Man would not tolerate such shenanigans in his place.

Without exchanging words, Pretty Man & Indigo came up with an arrangement. She was, after all, a Geechee Capitan, too. From that point on Indigo spent her time at Sneed's in the "social room," playing her fiddle. Since you could only buy liquor in bottles from sunup till sundown, coming over to Sneed's social room for a glass of beer or a shot of whiskey just made common sense to high-livers in Charleston.

Table service, some gambling, and that child on the fiddle were a gratifying combination after work for the family folks, and before work for the night labor force.

Indigo didn't change her style of playing. She still went after what she was feeling. But now she'd look at somebody. Say a brown-skinned man with a scar on his cheek, leathery hands, and a tiredness in his eyes. Then she'd bring her soul all up in his till she'd ferreted out the most lovely moment in that man's life. & she played that. You could tell from looking that as Indigo let notes fly from the fiddle, that man's scar wasn't quite so ugly; his eyes filling with energy, a tenderness tapping from those fingers now, just music. The slaves who were ourselves aided Indigo's mission, connecting soul & song, experience & unremembered rhythms. Pretty Man was relieved. Indigo'd found her a place. He could tell Uncle John there'd be no more wanton juvenile Circe in these parts. There was coming for sure a woman in charge of her powers. Training was what she was wanting.

Pretty Man didn't know how Indigo played what she played, but he did know she had a gift. Spats had mentioned how the girl couldn't play in her house 'less she agreed to take lessons. So a teacher for Indigo was out

of the question. There's more than one way to skin a cat,
& Pretty Man hadn't gotten this far 'cause of a lack of
imagination. No. There was something real simple that
he could do. Pretty Man liked the simple things in life:
money, a good woman, respect. Mabel, his girl, was a
simple sweet woman who helped out in the social room.
Pretty Man sent Mabel in her tight straight red skirt out
in the streets looking for any records with violin playing
on 'em. They were gonna replace the jukebox for a
while. "Yes," he said to himself, "Digo gonna play it by
ear, here, for a time. For some time."

Mabel, who was as dutiful as a southern girl could be,
came back from all the record stores with a peculiar
assortment of violin melodies & violinists. Yehudi Menu-
hin plays Bartók, *Violin Concerto #2*. Papa John Creach.
Duke Ellington's Jazz Violin Session with Svend As-
mussen, Stéphane Grappelli, Ray Nance, & Billy Stray-
horn. Heifetz plays Bach, *Unaccompanied Sonatas & Par-
titas*. Plus Stuff Smith. "I got one of every violiner they
had," Mabel cooed. Pretty Man looked at each album.
Nodded his head. "Get these on that ol' jukebox for me,
okay?" It was done.

Pretty Man offered Indigo a dollar for every one of the
tunes she learned to play by ear, or to play as the record
played. Pretty Man called everything from Bach to Ellington a tune. If it was Smith's "Blues in the Dungeon,"
that was a tune. Just as Bartók's 2nd movement, *andante
tranquillo*, was a tune. Indigo didn't jump at the chance
to change her aesthetic. In fact, she told Pretty Man
there was no sense at all in playing something that
somebody else could already play. But Spats & Crunch
had a meeting on the matter, determined that Indigo's
pursuits would mightily enhance the Jr. G.C. treasury.
Even Indigo didn't argue 'gainst that. Imagine all the
finery & catfish the Jr. Geechee Capitans could offer the

not-so-well-off Colored, now Christmas was coming. Indigo, indeed, had made her presence felt in the small
gang since her initiation. Give gifts to those who should
know love. Give hell to those who take us lightly. New
mottos. New priorities emerging for the Geechee Capitans.

Pretty Man gave Mabel change for the jukebox, whenever Indigo was training. Indigo didn't do badly. Yet the
nuance & dexterity of the masters occasionally eluded
her, her personal rhythms running contrary to theirs.
The octaves she chose, not the ones sounded by Creach
or Heifetz. Then, too, one time she forgot she wasn't to
take solos during Ellington's "Tricky Licks" and played
all on top of Ray Nance. Pretty Man was impressed by
Indigo's determination to rise up to the challenge. Mabel
was concerned, 'cause folks used to the child's fiddlin'
till they souls spoke, were getting cantankerous, leaving
early, not leaving tips, being genuinely unpleasant.
Missing something.

Late one afternoon when the social room was usually
crowded with menfolks & womenfolks, going on 'bout
the Colored, the day's doings, and what might be in the
cards, Mabel watched. Nothing going on but Indigo &
that jukebox. Violins. Violins. Violins, white folks done
come up from they grave to drive the Colored out of a
nice spot, they spot. All this fiddlin' was makin' folks
unhappy, not wanting no drinks, not wanting the hush
puppies, greens, & catfish Mabel prepared with so much
spice. All them empty tables. All them fiddles. It was
better before, when the girl played her own mind. There
was a fullness to conversation then. Plus, Pretty Man
spoke to her 'bout more than how was Indigo playing.
"What's the girl doing on her fiddle these days?" he'd
ask. Like all Mabel had to do was remember each time
she'd heard "Blues in C" or "Arabian Song, No. 42."

No. No. Mabel looked at Indigo sitting by the jukebox, listening, fingering, humming. No more. Mabel pulled the plug out the wall. Took a step toward Indigo. "Indigo, give me that fiddle. Right this minute, do you hear me? Pretty Man don't want no more fiddlin' round heah. Now, c'mon, give it heah." Indigo moved quick, like moonlight. "Spats. Crunch. *G.C. in trouble. G.C. in trouble.*" Indigo let the force of her own style of fiddle-fightin' come to the fore. Such a war-cry bouncing in the social room where hips & bosoms used to shake. Mabel was overwhelmed by her mission to have things be the way they used to be, not understanding that Indigo's existence made that impossible.

Spats & Crunch came running. Spats threw chairs in fronta Mabel's every step. Crunch kept Mabel's grabbing hands off Indigo's face & fiddle. Mabel took on the attributes of a lioness, prowling, growling. It was everything the boys could do to save Indigo; her hair or her fiddle.

Mabel proceeded to attack the boys with her nails, her heels, her teeth, her voice. She callt on everybody: Moses & her mother. "Jesus, get that fiddle out my life." Spats had some scratches. Crunch was generally a mess. They were all a little scared. Mabel was shouting for Pretty Man. Pretty Man was Mabel's man. They were in a lot of trouble.

Spats thought they should get on outta Sneed's. "My brother ain't gonna stand for us fightin' his woman." Fiddle in arm, Indigo clammered thru the caverns, Spats & Crunch beside her. "We in for it now. Damn we might haveta hide out, when Pretty Man know what we done!" Crunch's hearing wasn't subtle enough to catch Mabel's screams. Pretty Man having one of his tempers. Indigo slowed down. "We ain't the ones haveta run nowhere." Spats was impatient. "We got ta keep movin'." Crunch was already gone. Spats tried pulling Indigo by her free arm. "Digo, c'mon. We cain't let Pretty Man catch us. Let's go." Indigo shook her head. "No, I'ma go back & see to Mabel." & Spats was gone.

Indigo felt The Caverns for the first time. The air was dark, heavy. The baking breads wafted thru her nostrils, leaden. Her fiddle, as she let it fall over her side, weighed down on her spirit. Shame crawled up her cheeks. She was going to see about Mabel. Mabel had gotten in trouble 'cause of Indigo's fiddle, 'cause Indigo was a Geechee Capitan. Mabel was just some woman. One day Indigo would be a woman, too. The shame etched tears down her face, pushed her back toward the social room. Fear dashed her 'gainst the wall in the dark, when Pretty Man, as pretty as ever, briskly went up to the bakery. He was putting his shirt back in his pants as he walked, straightening himself up. Indigo wisht the switchblade handles on her violin case were knives. She'd have them all land in his back, but she didn't want to hurt anybody else. The Colored had been hurt enough already.

The Caverns began to moan, not with sorrow but in recognition of Indigo's revelation. The slaves who were ourselves had known terror intimately, confused sunrise with pain, & accepted indifference as kindness. Now they sang out from the walls, pulling Indigo toward them. Indigo ran her hands along the walls, to get the song, getta hold to the voices. Instead her fingers grazed cold, hard metal rings. Rust covered her palms & fingers. She kept following the rings. Chains. Leg irons. The Caverns revealed the plight of her people, but kept on singing. The tighter Indigo held the chains in her hands, the less shame was her familiar. Mabel's tiny woeful voice hovered over the blood thick chorus of The Caverns. Indigo knew her calling. The Colored had hurt enough already.

EMERGENCY CARE OF OPEN WOUNDS /
WHEN IT HURTS
by Indigo

Calmly rinse the wound with copious amounts of cold tap water. This will significantly reduce the possibilities of infection. If available, use clean linen applied firmly against the wound to inhibit bleeding. If the pressure is not adequate, do it again. Another method allows the bottom of a stainless-steel saucepan to be applied to the wound. The cold of the pan reduces swelling as well as bleeding. A poultice of mandrake berries can be of great use also, until further care can be offered.

EMERGENCY CARE OF WOUNDS THAT
CANNOT BE SEEN

Hold the victim gently. Rock in the manner of a quiet sea. Hum softly from your heart. Repeat the victim's name with love. Offer a brew of red sunflower to cleanse the victim's blood & spirit. Fasting & silence for a time refurbish the victim's awareness of her capacity to nourish & heal herself. New associations should be made with caution, more caring for herself.

Indigo carefully wrapped her dolls in sheets of white cotton she'd borrowed from her mother's weaving rooms. To the left of the moon she'd painted on her wall was a growing mound of white ovals with little cloth feet sticking out. The sun was fading. Fine tints of orange lingered on the edges of the dolls' heads, which all pointed to the east. Indigo had wrapped Marie-Hélène &

Miranda last. Hugging them both, kissing their fore-
heads, holding them at arms' length to get one final
glimpse of those who had been her closest friends. After
a final curtsey to the shrouded companions, Indigo
played what she remembered of Bartók. Each note demanding precision, honesty, and depth.

Lord, this child is a miracle, thought her mother,
Hilda Effania, as she listened & watched from the door.
She'd stolen up the back stairs as quickly as she could
when she'd heard *real* music coming from Indigo's
room. Yet now she felt a regret that she'd forbidden the
child her willful desire to play her soul. It was true like
Aunt Haydee said, "A youngun'll come up with what
you want, when ya leave 'em the room to find it." Indigo
finished all the lyrical fragments she could from heart,
plus she'd added a tag from "Cotton Tail." Bowing very
formally, *legato,* Indigo turned to put her fiddle in its
case. She saw her mother, hesitated, and stammered,
"Mama, I think it's time I stopped playing with dolls,
don't you?"

"Well, I do recall sayin' something like that one of
those terribly busy days, when I already had my hands
full. Musta been the day you wanted a 'period' dinner . . ."

"No, a menstruation dinner, Mama."

"That's right, I do believe I tol' you to pack 'em up
in the attic." Hilda Effania bit her lips, smuggled a smile
out of her concern for her child. "Indigo, you don't
haveta bury the girls. I think they look wonderful here
in your room. As long as I can remember, you've gone
to bed with your dollies. No matter how angry I was
when I said what I said, you know I don't hold a soul
to my every word. You keep your dolls as long as you
want. Why, I think at least Miranda can come to Christmas dinner." Hilda Effania wanted Indigo to lose this

forlorn curve in her back, the sadness in her gaze. But Indigo was resolute.

"No, Mama. I don't think they're quite dead, they're just resting, I think." Indigo looked up at her mama wanting very much. All she said was: "Mama, I couldn't bear for them to grow up. I couldn't stand it, Mama. I just couldn't."

Hilda Effania really didn't know what was the matter. She knew to hold Indigo close to her, to say her name over & over till the child was ready to talk.

"Mama, it's hard, isn't it?"

"What's hard, Indigo?"

"Being a grown colored woman is hard, ain't it? Just like you tol' me. Just 'cause I haveta grow up, my dolls don't haveta. I can save them. Mama, let's take them to the attic. You & me. I don't even wanta invite Mrs. Yancey, though Miranda will miss her. Just you & me, let's do something very special."

Hilda Effania sat Indigo down on the bed with her. She rocked her baby in her arms, patted her back, hummed a tune as she made it up.

"I don't know that it's all that hard to be a full-grown colored woman, Indigo. I can imagine not wanting your friends to grow up, though. If they grow up, eventually, they will haveta go. But, you know they could stay little girls forever."

"How, Mama?"

"You know it's Christmas time, & there's hundreds of other little girls, oh tiny little girls, who'd take real good care of Miranda, Marie-Hélène & all the rest of them. & you & I know there's no dollies in the whole world quite like these." Hilda Effania tried so hard not to laugh. She had flashes of Indigo stealing rice from the kitchen, buttons from the sewing room, bits of satin from patterns for Miz Fitzhugh's ball gowns. "Like I was saying, Indigo, there's no dollies like this anywhere on the earth."

"You mean, give 'em away to strangers?" Indigo asked, indignant.

"You said they weren't dead, just resting," Hilda Effania responded, while she put Indigo's Stetson on her head. "You know, for a man's hat, that's pretty sharp, Indigo."

Indigo pulled the hat off her head, thought a second. Stood in front of her mother with a desperate air.

"Mama, I'll make the other lil girls new dollies, honest I will. I promise. But I want you & me to have a ceremony for my dollies & let em rest till I have a baby, or till Cypress or Sassafrass has a baby. Please Mama, I want them to stay with the family."

It was true. After Indigo there'd be no more babies in the family till one of her girls was grown enough to bring one home. Hilda Effania couldn't agree more with Indigo's familial fervor. After all, she was devoted to her daughters. Now, Indigo, all of 12, was saving her most treasured possessions for the daughters to come. This made sense to Hilda Effania, who'd seen those other two grow up much too fast. This was the day that Indigo caught up with them.

"Okay, what sort of ceremony do you want to have?"

"I want you to sing some holy song, while I carry them one by one to the attic. That's what I wanta do, Mama. Then I wanta come downstairs & help you make the gumbo for when Cypress & Sassafrass come home. Can I, please?" Indigo was excited, beginning & ending the largest segment of her life.

Hilda Effania changed her clothes once she got in the spirit of things. She put on a crêpe dress with pearls & black velvet round the shoulders, a little lipstick, some mascara. At her suggestion, Indigo put on her white taffeta Communion dress. Hilda Effania stationed herself

at the foot of the second-floor stairs leading to the attic.
Indigo solemnly carried each doll up the curving steps,
as her mother's voice rose behind her to the rafters:

> *"Jesus lover of my soul*
> *Hide me, oh my Savior*
> *Hide me till the storm of life is past*
> *While the stormy waters roll*
> *While the tempest still is high."*

"Mama, this gumbo is ridiculous." Sassafrass was eating so fast she could barely get the words out of her mouth. "Mama, you know if I told them white folks at the Callahan School that I wanted some red sauce & rice with shrimp, clams, hot sausage, corn, okra, chicken & crab meat, they'd go round the campus sayin, 'You know that Negro girl overdoes everything. Can you imagine what she wanted for dinner?'" Cypress was at the side board of the sink doing *pliés* which Sassafrass' story had interrupted.

"Hey S., don't tell no more jokes. I can't do my exercises."

"I helped Mama make that gumbo, Sassafrass. I'm so glad you like it," chirped Indigo at the table, working on a doll for some little girl her mother said Santa wouldn't be visiting.

Hilda Effania was ecstatic. All her girls were home. Cypress was back from studying dance in New York. Sassafrass had made that terrible bus trip from New England. As much as they'd changed she still recognized them as her children. Spinning in the kitchen, while her girls did whatever they were going to do, was her most precious time.

From her corner view, she could see everyone. Sassafrass was still eating & still heavy hipped. If the white folks' food was so awful, you sure couldn't tell it. On the other hand, Cypress was too thin round her waist. It was as if she was rejecting the body the Lord gave her. There is nothing can be done with a colored behind. Hilda knew Cypress was so determined to be a ballet dancer she'd starve, but never lose that backside. Indigo was making every effort to be in on the big girls' talk. Hilda spun her fleece. Later, they'd all help her dye, warp, & weave. They always did.

"Sassafrass, it's 'those' white folks, not 'them.' Cypress, your sister's name is Sassafrass, not 'S.' "

In the midst of an *arabesque penché* Cypress retorted, "So tell me something I don't know."

Hilda Effania took a deep breath, sighed quite loudly. These northern ways would haveta be quieted. "I'm sorry, Cypress, I don't think I heard what you said." Cypress returned to first position, *bras en répos.*

"Aw, Mama, that's a turn of phrase. You know, some slang."

"Sounded like a fresh somebody to me," Hilda said, without loosing the gait of her spinning.

"Vocabulary is simply a way of knowing & letting others know your intentions. That's what Madame says." Cypress executed a *croisé devant,* balanced, smiled.

"& does Madame encourage you to insult your mother?" Hilda went on. Sassafrass was looking very bored, though Cypress kept trying to impress them with her new skills: *rond de jambe en l'air; gargouillade; cabriole, brisé.* Repeating the words, with each movement.

"Cypress, do you speak English anymore? Or has everyone in New York learned French in deference to the ballet?" Indigo laughed. Hilda smiled inside. Cypress relaxed her body & looked more like herself to Hilda.

"Mama, would you explain to my sister from the woods that I was trying to offer her some culture."

"She's right there. You can tell her."

"Cypress, I am going to a school where culture is never mentioned, per se, because all those white folks up there is 'culture,' or so they'd like us to believe." Sassafrass leaned back in her chair. Cypress was right. What she was doing was so pretty. Cypress was in her own way offering a gift.

"Cypress, could you show me some of that? I mean, how you do that? Those WASPs don't look like you when they do it. You make it look so easy."

"Show me too. I wanta know too." Indigo stuck a needle in the bosom of the dollie & stood up, ready for her first lesson at the *barre.*

Hilda wisht her husband Alfred could see the girls lined up by the kitchen sink, taking a ballet lesson from Cypress, while Sassafrass recited Dunbar. They were so much his children: hard-headed, adventurous, dreamers. Hilda Effania had some dreams of her own. Not so much to change the world, but to change her daughters' lives. Make it so they wouldn't have to do what she did. Listen to every syllable come out that white woman's mouth. It wasn't really distasteful to her. She liked her life. She liked making cloth: the touch, the rhythm of it, colors. What she wanted for her girls was more than that. She wanted happiness, however they could get it. Whatever it was. Whoever brought it.

"Oh. I can't imagine how I forgot. I think that Skippie Schuyler boy is having a party on Christmas Eve. & I do believe there's an invitation on the table by the front door."

57/

"Skippie Schuyler, the doctor's son, invited us, Mama?"

"Well, I don't see why not. You're getting better training & education than anybody else in Charleston. You certainly are the prettiest girls I've seen round here for a long time."

Sassafrass ran to get the invitation. Firm white paper with gold printing.

Eugene Alphonso Schuyler, III
invites
Sassafrass, Cypress & Indigo
to a
Christmas Eve Wassail

Six to Nine O'Clock   *Chaperoned/R.S.V.P.*

Indigo jumped up & down. "Mama, Mama, he invited me! Me! He doesn't even know me!"

"No, but he might have heard there was a beautiful child gone astray with those Geechee Capitans," Hilda remarked.

Sassafrass & Cypress looked hard at Indigo. "You've been being a what?" Cypress screeched.

"A Jr. G.C., but I resigned. I resigned."

"Well, I don't see anything so bad about it, Mama. She'll never meet those kinds of fellas at Eugene Alphonso Schuyler III's house. Thank God for the colored people."

"Sassafrass, are you crazy? Indigo can't be runnin' the streets with those hoodlums." Cypress was incensed with her sister's cavalier attitude. Those kinds of fellas killed people, maimed people. She'd seen it where she lived on the Lower East Side.

"Look, Cypress, except for some rich little colored boys just like Skippie at our 'Brother' school, I haven't seen any Negroes in over 5 months. Any Negro whose color don't wash off is a treasure now. Believe me."

"But, I said I had resigned. I want to go to Skippie's party. Really I do." Indigo couldn't understand the tension between her sisters. What was the matter? They were all going. Then Indigo remembered the Wheeler girls. Those skinny yellow girls.

They were more like honey in a wolf's body, arsenic in a chocolate. As a Jr. G.C., Indigo'd put those children in their places. What would they do, if she were at a party with them?

Sassafrass just wanted to go. Some Negroes. Three hours of solid Negro conversation. Not having to explain to anybody what it was she actually meant. A dance. A dance with somebody who knew the rhythm of the song. A hand that was not afraid to touch hers. She wanted to go.

Cypress kept saying the word "wassail" over & over in her mind. " 'Wassail' has nothing to do with where I've been. I don't think. 'Wassail' is non-alcoholic for these children. How can Mama expect me to go have some wassail with some rich little colored children. I'd rather see a grown man or *Giselle.* "

Hilda Effania knew her children. She knew Indigo was a little nervous that her escapades with Spats & Crunch would spoil her entry to society. She knew Sassafrass didn't give a damn what kind of Colored she saw, so long as she saw a colored somebody. She knew Cypress knew too much.

Indigo's freshly curled & pressed hair was standing all over her head when she came in the door. "Mama, I danced with Charlie, Edward, Butch, Skippie himself, and Philip."

"That's not all she did, Mother. She invited Spats & Crunch into the Schuylers' house," Cypress slurred. "They seemed to have a good time, with their hats on."

"Oh, they did. We all did. Didn't we, Sassafrass?" Sassafrass was on the porch tongue-kissing Skippie Schuyler's second cousin from Richmond, who was also a doctor's son.

"Mama, you know none of the Wheeler girls had on a specially made for them dress. Can you believe that?"

Hilda Effania gave Cypress one of those looks that means you-&-I-will-talk-later. That child had gotta hold of some liquor somewhere. In the meantime, Hilda Effania was experiencing being tickled. Her girls were great successes. They knew. Everybody else knew it. She knew it. She tried to be very serious as she called Sassafrass in from the porch, but it was all so exciting. Sassafrass finally came in from the cold.

"Aw, Mama, isn't love wonderful?"

Cypress stood in the corner doing *battements* with the grace of a panther. "Mama, I want to go back to New York."

"Mama, I think I need to go see Aunt Haydee. She tol' me one time that all I had to do was watch the moon. & I couldn't even see the moon tonight."

"Don't worry 'bout that, darling. Tomorrow we'll all have our Christmas. We'll see what we have to do, after Santa pays us a visit."

"Aw Mama, not Santa Claus." All three together.

"Yes. Santa Claus." Hilda Effania gave a hot toddy & a piece of pound cake to each & every one. She listened to the five & ten minute courtships her daughters recounted.

"& then he said . . . you know what Billy said to me,

I know I was chosen . . . Go on, Mama, guess what happened then . . ."

Hilda Effania couldn't wait till Christmas. The Christ Child was born. Hallelujah. Hallelujah. The girls were home. The house was humming. Hilda Effania just a singing, cooking up a storm. Up before dawn. Santa's elves barely up the chimney. She chuckled. This was gonna be some mornin'. Yes, indeed. There was nothing too good for her girls. Matter of fact, what folks never dreamt of would only just about do. That's right, all her babies home for Christmas Day. Hilda Effania cooking up a storm. Little Jesus Child lyin' in his Manger. Praise the Lord for all these gifts. Hilda Effania justa singin':

Poor little Jesus Child, Born in a Manger
Sweet little Jesus Child
& they didn't know who you were.

BREAKFAST WITH HILDA EFFANIA & HER GIRLS ON CHRISTMAS MORNING

Hilda's Turkey Hash

1 pound diced cooked turkey meat (white & dark)
2 medium onions, diced
1 red sweet pepper, diced
1 full boiled potato, diced

1 tablespoon cornstarch
3 tablespoons butter
Salt to taste, pepper too
(A dash of corn liquor, optional)

In a heavy skillet, put your butter. Sauté your onions & red pepper. Add your turkey, once your onions are transparent.

When the turkey's sizzling, add your potato. Stir. If consistency is not to your liking, add the cornstarch to thicken, the corn liquor to thin. Test to see how much salt & pepper you want. & don't forget your cayenne.

Catfish/ The Way Albert Liked It

½ cup flour	3 beaten eggs
½ cup cornmeal	Oil for cooking
Salt	Lemons
Pepper	6 fresh catfish
½ cup buttermilk	

Sift flour and cornmeal. Season with your salt & pepper. Mix the beaten eggs well with the buttermilk. Dip your fish in the egg & milk. Then roll your fish in the cornmeal-flour mix. Get your oil spitting hot in a heavy skillet. Fry your fish, not too long, on both sides. Your lemon wedges are for your table.

Trio Marmalade

1 tangerine	Sugar
1 papaya	Cold water
1 lemon	

Delicately grate rinds of fruits. Make sure you have slender pieces of rind. Chop up your pulp, leaving the middle section of each fruit. Put the middles of the fruits and the seeds some-where else in a cotton wrap. Add three times the amount of pulp & rind. That's the measure for your water. Keep this sitting overnight. Get up the next day & boil this for a half hour. Drop your wrapped seed bag in there. Boil that, too. & mix in an exact equal of your seed bag with your sugar (white or brown). Leave it be for several hours. Come back. Get it boiling again. Don't stop stirring. You can test it & test it, but you'll know when it jells. Put on your table or in jars you seal while it's hot.

Now you have these with your hominy grits. (I know you know how to make hominy grits.) Fried eggs, sunny-side-up. Ham-sliced bacon, butter rolls, & Aunt Haydee's Red Pimiento Jam. I'd tell you that receipt, but Aunt Haydee never told nobody how it is you make that. I keep a jar in the pantry for special occasions. I get one come harvest.

Mama's breakfast simmering way downstairs drew the girls out of their sleep. Indigo ran to the kitchen. Sassafrass turned back over on her stomach to sleep a while longer, there was no House Mother ringing a cow bell. Heaven. Cypress brushed her hair, began her daily *pliés* & leg stretches. Hilda Effania sat at her kitchen table, drinking strong coffee with Magnolia Milk, wondering what the girls would think of her tree.

"Merry Christmas, Mama." Indigo gleamed. "May I please have some coffee with you? Nobody else is up yet. Then we can go see the tree, can't we, when they're all up. Should I go get 'em?" Indigo was making herself this coffee as quickly as she could, before Hilda Effania said "no." But Hilda was so happy Indigo could probably have had a shot of bourbon with her coffee.

"Only half a cup, Indigo. Just today." Hilda watched Indigo moving more like Cypress. Head erect, back stretched tall, with some of Sassafrass' easy coyness.

"So you had a wonderful time last night at your first party?"

"Oh, yes, Mama." Indigo paused. "But you know what?" Indigo sat down by her mother with her milk tinged with coffee. She stirred her morning treat, serious as possible. She looked her mother in the eyes. "Mama, I don't think boys are as much fun as everybody says."

"What do you mean, darling?"

"Well, they dance. & I guess eventually you marry 'em. But I like my fiddle so much more. I even like my dolls better than boys. They're fun, but they can't talk about important things."

Hilda Effania giggled. Indigo was making her own path at her own pace. There'd be not one more boy-crazy, obsessed-with-romance child in her house. This last one made more sense out of the world than either of the other two. Alfred would have liked that. He liked independence.

"Good morning, Mama. Merry Christmas." Sassafrass was still tying her bathrobe as she kissed her mother.

"Merry Christmas, Indigo. I see Santa left you a cup of coffee."

"This is not my first cup of coffee. I had some on my birthday, too."

"Oh, pardon me. I didn't realize you were so grown. I've been away, you know?" Sassafrass was never very pleasant in the morning. Christmas was no exception. Indigo & her mother exchanged funny faces. Sassafrass wasn't goin' to spoil this day.

"Good morning. Good morning. Good morning, everyone." Cypress flew through the kitchen: *coupé jeté en tournant.*

"Merry Christmas, Cypress," the family shouted in unison.

"Oh, Mama, you musta been up half the night cooking what all I'm smelling." Cypress started lifting pot tops, pulling the oven door open.

"Cypress, you know I can't stand for nobody to be looking in my food till I serve it. Now, come on away from my stove."

Cypress turned to her mama, smiling. "Mama, let's go look at the tree."

"I haven't finished my coffee," Sassafrass yawned.

"You can bring it with you. That's what I'm gonna do," Indigo said with sweet authority.

The tree glistened by the front window of the parlor. Hilda Effania had covered it, of course, with cloth & straw. Satin ribbons of scarlet, lime, fuchsia, bright yellow, danced on the far limbs of the pine. Tiny straw angels of dried palm swung from the upper branches. Apples shining, next to candy canes & gingerbread men, brought shouts of joy & memory from the girls, who recognized their own handiwork. The black satin stars with appliqués of the Christ Child Cypress had made when she was ten. Sassafrass fingered the lyres she fashioned for the children singing praises of the little Jesus: little burlap children with lyres she'd been making since she could thread a needle, among the miniatures of Indigo's dolls. Hilda Effania had done something else special for this Christmas, though. In silk frames of varied pastels were the baby pictures of her girls, & one of her wedding day: Hilda Effania & Alfred, November 30, 1946.

Commotion. Rustling papers. Glee & Surprise. Indigo got a very tiny laced brassiere from Cypress. Sassafrass had given her a tiny pair of earrings, dangling golden violins. Indigo had made for both her sisters dolls in their very own likenesses. Both five feet tall, with hips, & bras. Indigo had dressed the dolls in the old clothes Cypress & Sassafrass had left at home.

"Look in their panties," Indigo blurted. Cypress felt down in her doll's panties. Sassafrass pulled her doll's drawers. They both found velvet sanitary napkins with their names embroidered cross the heart of silk.

"Oh, Indigo. You're kidding. You're not menstruating, are you?"

"Indigo, you got your period?"

"Yes, she did." Hilda Effania joined, trying to change

the subject. She'd known Indigo was making dolls, but not that the dolls had their period.

"Well, what else did you all get?" Hilda asked provocatively.

Cypress pulled out an oddly shaped package wrapped entirely in gold sequins. "Mama, this is for you." The next box was embroidered continuously with Sassafrass' name. "Here, guess whose?" Cypress held Indigo's shoulders. Indigo had on her new bra over her night-gown. Waiting for her mother & sister to open their gifts, Cypress did *tendues*. "Hold still, Indigo. If you move, my alignment goes off."

"Oh, Cypress, this is just lovely." Hilda Effania didn't know what else to say. Cypress had given her a black silk negligée with a very revealing bed jacket. "I certainly have to think when I could wear this. & you all won't be home to see it."

"Aw, Mama. Try it on," Cypress pleaded.

"Yeah, Mama. Put that on. It looks so nasty." Indigo squinched up her face, giggled.

"Oh, Cypress, these are so beautiful. I can hardly believe it." Sassafrass held the embroidered box open. In the box lined with beige raw silk were 7 cherrywood hand-carved crochet needles of different gauges.

"Bet not one white girl up to the Callahan School has ever in her white life laid eyes on needles like that!" Cypress hugged her sister, flexed her foot. "In-digo, you got to put that bra on under your clothes, not on top of 'em! Mama, would you look at this little girl?"

Hilda Effania had disappeared. "I'm trying on this scandalous thing, Cypress. You all look for your notes at the foot of the tree." She shouted from her bedroom, thinking she looked pretty good for a widow with three most grown girls.

Sassafrass, Cypress & Indigo

Hilda Effania always left notes for the girls, explaining where their Christmas from Santa was. This practice began the first year Sassafrass had doubted that a fat white man came down her chimney to bring her anything. Hilda solved that problem by leaving notes from Santa Claus for all the children. That way they had to go search the house, high & low, for their gifts. Santa surely had to have been there. Once school chums & reality interfered with this myth, Hilda continued the practice of leaving her presents hidden away. She liked the idea that each child experienced her gift in privacy. The special relationship she nurtured with each was protected from rivalries, jokes, & Christmas confusions. Hilda Effania loved thinking that she'd managed to give her daughters a moment of their own.

My Oldest Darling, Sassafrass,
 In the back of the pantry is
something from Santa. In a red box
by the attic window is something your
father would want you to have. Out
by the shed in a bucket covered with
straw is a gift from your Mama.
                    Love to you,
                         Mama

Darling Cypress,
 Underneath my hat boxes in the
2nd floor closet is your present from
Santa. Look behind the tomatoes I
canned last year for what I got you
in your Papa's name. My own choice
for you is under your bed.
                    XOXOX,
                         Mama

Sweet Little Indigo,
  This is going to be very simple.
Santa left you something outside your
violin. I left you a gift by the outdoor
stove on the right hand side. Put your
coat on before you go out there. And
the special something I got you from
your Daddy is way up in the china
cabinet. Please, be careful.
    I love you so much,
        Mama

In the back of the pantry between the flour & rice, Sassafrass found a necklace of porcelain roses. Up in the attic across from Indigo's mound of resting dolls, there was a red box all right, with a woven blanket of mohair, turquoise & silver. Yes, her father would have wanted her to have a warm place to sleep. Running out to the shed, Sassafrass knocked over the bucket filled with straw. There on the ground lay eight skeins of her mother's finest spun cotton, dyed so many colors. Sassafrass sat out in the air feeling her yarns.

Cypress wanted her mother's present first. Underneath her bed, she felt tarlatan. A tutu. Leave it to Mama. Once she gathered the whole thing out where she could see it, Cypress started to cry. A tutu *juponnage,* reaching to her ankles, rose & lavender. The waist was a wide sash with the most delicate needlework she'd ever seen. Tiny toe shoes in white & pink graced brown ankles tied with ribbons. Unbelievable. Cypress stayed in her room dancing in her tutu till lunchtime. Then she found *The Souls of Black Folks* by DuBois near the tomatoes from her Papa's spirit. She was the only one who'd insisted on calling him Papa, instead of Daddy or Father. He didn't mind. So she guessed he wouldn't mind now. "Thank you so much, Mama & Papa." Cypress slowly went to the 2nd floor closet where she found Santa'd left her a pair of opal earrings. To thank her mother Cypress did a complete *port de bras*, in the Cecchetti manner, by her mother's vanity. The mirrors inspired her.

Indigo had been very concerned that anything was near her fiddle that she hadn't put there. Looking at her violin, she knew immediately what her gift from Santa was. A brand-new case. No second-hand battered thing from Uncle John. Indigo approached her instrument slowly. The case was of crocodile skin, lined with white velvet. Plus, Hilda Effania had bought new rosin, new strings. Even cushioned the fiddle with cleaned raw wool. Indigo carried her new case with her fiddle outside to the stove where she found a music stand holding *A Practical Method for Violin* by Nicolas Laoureux. "Oh, my. She's right about that. Mama would be real mad if I never learned to read music." Indigo looked thru the pages, understanding nothing. Whenever she was dealing with something she didn't understand, she made it her business to learn. With great difficulty, she carried her fiddle, music stand, & music book into the house. Up behind the wine glasses that Hilda Effania rarely used, but dusted regularly, was a garnet bracelet from the memory of her father. Indigo figured the bracelet weighed so little, she would definitely be able to wear it every time she played her fiddle. Actually, she could wear it while conversing with the Moon.

Hilda Effania decided to chance fate & spend the rest of the morning in her fancy garb from Cypress. The girls were silent when she entered the parlor in black lace. She looked like she did in those hazy photos from before they were born. Indigo rushed over to the easy chair & straightened the pillows.

"Mama, I have my present for you." Hilda Effania swallowed hard. There was no telling what Indigo might bring her.

"Well, Sweetheart. I'm eager for it. I'm excited, too."

Indigo opened her new violin case, took out her violin, made motions of tuning it (which she'd already done). In a terribly still moment, she began "My Buddy," Hilda Effania's mother's favorite song. At the end, she bowed to her mother. Her sisters applauded.

Sassafrass gave her mother two things: a woven hanging of twined ikat using jute and raffia, called "You Know Where We Came From, Mama"; & six amethysts with holes drilled thru, for her mother's creative weaving.

"Mama, you've gotta promise me you won't have a bracelet, or a ring or something made from them. Those are for your very own pieces." Sassafrass wanted her mother to experience weaving as an expression of herself, not as something the family did for Miz Fitzhugh. Hilda Effania was still trying to figure out where in the devil she could put this "hanging," as Sassafrass called it.

"Oh, no dear. I wouldn't dream of doing anything with these stones but what you intended."

When the doorbell rang, Hilda Effania didn't know what to do with herself. Should she run upstairs? Sit calmly? Run get her house robe? She had no time to do any of that. Indigo opened the door.

"Merry Christmas, Miz Fitzhugh. Won't you come in?" Hilda sank back in the easy chair. Cypress casually threw her mother an afghan to cover herself. Miz Fitzhugh in red wool suit, tailored green satin shirt, red tam, all Hilda's design, and those plain brown pumps white women like, wished everyone a "Merry Christmas." She said Mathew, her butler, would bring some sweetbreads & venison over later, more toward the dinner hour. Miz Fitzhugh liked Sassafrass the best of the girls. That's why she'd sponsored her at the Callahan School. The other two, the one with the gall to want to be a ballerina & the headstrong one with the fiddle, were much too much for Miz Fitzhugh. They didn't even wanta be weavers. What was becoming of the Negro, refusing to ply an honorable trade.

Nevertheless, Miz Fitzhugh hugged each one with her frail blue-veined arms, gave them their yearly checks for their savings accounts she'd established when each was born. There be no talk that her Negroes were destitute. What she didn't know was that Hilda Effania let the girls use that money as they pleased. Hilda believed every family needed only one mother. She was the mother to her girls. That white lady was mighty generous, but she wasn't her daughters' mama or manna from Heaven. If somebody needed taking care of, Hilda Effania determined that was her responsibility; knowing in her heart that white folks were just peculiar.

"Why Miz Fitzhugh, that's right kindly of you," Hilda honeyed.

"Why Hilda, you know I feel like the girls were my very own," Miz Fitzhugh confided. Cypress began a series of violent *ronds de jambe*. Sassafrass picked up all the wrapping papers as if it were the most important thing in the world. Indigo felt some huge anger coming over her. Next thing she knew, Miz Fitzhugh couldn't keep her hat on. There was a wind justa pushing, blowing Miz Fitzhugh out the door. Because she had blue blood or blue veins, whichever, Indigo knew Miz Fitzhugh would never act like anything strange was going on. She'd let herself be blown right out the door with her white kid gloves, red tailored suit, & all. Waving good-bye, shouting, "Merry Christmas," Miz Fitzhugh vanished as demurely as her station demanded.

71/

Ntozake Shange

Sucha raucous laughing & carrying on rarely came out of Hilda Effania's house like it did after Miz Fitzhugh'd been blown away. Hilda Effania did an imitation of her, hugging the girls.

"But Miz Fitzhugh, do the other white folks know you touch your Negroes?" Hilda responded, "Oh, I don't tell anyone!"

Eventually they all went to their rooms, to their private fantasies & preoccupations. Hilda was in the kitchen working the fat off her goose, fiddling with the chestnut stuffing, wondering how she would handle the house when it was really empty again. It would be empty, not even Indigo would be home come January.

"Yes, Alfred. I think I'm doing right by 'em. Sassafrass is in that fine school with rich white children. Cypress is studying classical ballet with Effie in New York City. Imagine that? I'm sending Indigo out to Difuskie with Aunt Haydee. Miz Fitzhugh's promised me a tutor for her. She doesn't want the child involved in all this violence 'bout the white & the colored going to school together, the integration. I know you know what I mean, 'less up there's segregated too.

"No, Alfred I'm not blaspheming. I just can't imagine another world. I'm trying to, though. I want the girls to live the good life. Like what we planned. Nice husbands. Big houses. Children. Trips to Paris & London. Going to the opera. Knowing nice people for friends. Remember we used to say we were the nicest, most interesting folks we'd ever met? Well, I don't want it to be that way for our girls. You know, I'm sort of scared of being here by myself. I can always talk to you, though. Can't I?

"I'ma tell Miz Fitzhugh that if she wants Indigo in Difuskie that tutor will have to be a violin teacher. Oh, Alfred, you wouldn't believe what she can do on that fiddle. If you could only see how Cypress dances. Sassa-

72/

frass' weavings. I wish you were here sometimes, so we could tell the world to look at what all we, Hilda Effania & Alfred, brought to this world."

Once her Christmas supper was organized in the oven, the frigerator, the sideboard, Hilda Effania slept in her new negligée, Alfred's WWII portrait close to her bosom.

My Littlest Angel, Indigo,

I've been making preserves to send to my girls, some canned tomatoes & pickles too. You know, I have to stay busy, even though the Lord knows I would be a mighty big somebody if I ever ate all that I sat up cooking. Meanwhile, I miss you all so much. There's times in a mother's life that are simply trying times. I've prayed & thought a whole lot 'bout my life & yours. Wouldn't I look simple, keeping a house full of grown women, aching to be part of the world, from being part of the world, just so I wouldn't be quite so lonely. That's enough of that. You all have your 'mends to make with the world & so do I. That's the Lord's way.

I heard from Sassafrass that she hitch-hiked all the way across the country, when she told me she was gonna "drive-away." That child is a mess. I'm up at night worrying 'bout her wanton ways. But she's finally in Los Angeles, & settling down a bit, I hope. I keep looking for Cypress' face to be on the news, when they talk about those youngsters who've lost their minds in California. I swear, I feel in my soul that she's wandering around San Francisco all painted up with stars & peace symbols. I pray the TV cameras never find her. She might do a dance, then what would I say to all my neighbors. I got a painted dancing daughter in Haight-Ashbury? (smile) You are such a comfort to me. You've always been so serious & thoughtful. I want you to keep your head on your shoulders, & try not to be so hard on your sisters. They aren't frivolous. They're just a little wild.

If you don't mind my saying, you're entitled to more fun than you allow yourself. Aunt Haydee's never been one for entertaining. If she gets a nap 'tween all those women out there having babies everytime you turn your back, it's a miracle. Now, that I'm thinking about it, you might enjoy having a baby of your own more than delivering everybody else's. That does not mean for you to take up with one of those island boys either! I am concentrating on a nice young man here in Charleston. You really should have been a doctor. No sense in being a nurse with all the experience you've had by now.

The Lord will set you upon a path of decent pleasures, sure as He makes a way for honest toil. Saints be praised, Indigo, I've got to run. The strawberries are boiling over. I do love all of you so much. Rushing away, now.

Love,
Mama

*N*othing but tenor sax solos ever came out of that house. Sometimes you could hear a man and a woman arguing, but almost always some kind of music. Sassafrass and Mitch lived together in that house, sort of hidden behind untended hedges and the peeling shingles. Even though they were living in L.A., there were always some dried leaves lying all across their stoop. Sassafrass thought it was the spirits, bringing them good luck; Mitch thought it was because she didn't ever sweep. But there was still the music, and the black Great Dane, Albert, whose real name was My-Name-Is-Albert-Ayler. None of the neighbors knew the dog's full name, so Sassafrass never worried about him being stolen because he only came when someone called his whole name. Sassafrass had named him after the screenplay she had started after the album she had made, and after her lover she never met . . . Albert Ayler was found in the East River. That was one of the reasons Mitch was attracted to her, because she had named her dog so irreverently after his mentor, alto-saxist Ayler. Still, Sassafrass was so full of love she couldn't call anybody anything without bringing good vibes from a whole lot of spirits to everything she touched.

Walter Cronkite's voice could be heard through the open window next to Sassafrass' bed. She was sitting there in a long blue and red cotton skirt, crocheting another hat for Mitch. The long walls of the fallen-down, almost Victorian house were totally covered with murals of African exploits. Every time the landlady came to repair the falling plaster on the ceiling she'd look so uncomfortable; her redneck lips would get littler than a needle and her cheeks would get all stiff. Sassafrass loved watching that old peckerwood get nervous from total blackness all through the house. The old peckerwood got $100.00 a month for the whole flat, which Sassafrass and Mitch had worked on to be a permanent monument to the indelibility of black creative innovation. She glanced up from her sixty-sixth stitch to see if there was anything else to do to the house to make it the most perfect place for her and Mitch to stay in until the black revolution, or until they moved to the black artists' and craftsmen's commune starting up just outside New Orleans, and pretty near a black nationalist settlement. Sassafrass believed it was absolutely necessary to take black arts out of the white man's hands; to take black people out of the white man's hands. But here she was in Highland Park, Los Angeles, with rednecks and Chicanos, because Mitch's parole officer refused to grant permission for them to live in any black area—and because they could only afford $100.00 a month—and because they didn't have the money to buy into the artists' commune near New Orleans anyhow: almost one thousand dollars, cash. So Sassafrass looked around to see if there was something else she could make to make them feel more like loving each other and hitting sunrise with hope, instead of the groans and crabbiness that ate through them toward the end of every poor month.

There were the exasperating patchwork curtains she had managed to get done, and macrame hangings in every doorway—one named for each of their heroes. There was the long and knotted purple jute, hanging for Malcolm, who was a king. It had bullets woven through the ends of it, and dried sand covered twigs passing in and out of the center. "Bullets and land of our own," Sassafrass had said, standing on Mitch's shoulders to hang it. Then there were the ones for Fidel, Garvey, Archie Shepp, and Coltrane. In her study, Sassafrass had sequestered a sequin-and-feather hanging shaped like a vagina, for Josephine Baker, but Mitch had made her hide it because it wasn't proper for a new Afrikan woman to make things of such a sexual nature. Just as she was remembering Mitch's tirade against her feather-work, Sassafrass felt the doors open and there he was— the cosmic lover and wonder of wonders to her: Mitch.

Mitch had to stoop a little under the doorway; he was almost seven feet tall, and long limbed like a Watusi with Ethiopian eyes that arched like rainbows, and gold earrings in both ears, etched real fine because they were from Mexico (antiques). His nose was slightly hooked like Nasser's, and his presence was that of one of those Olmec gods. Mitch thought of himself as a god, and he was always telling Sassafrass not to succumb to her mortality; to live like she was one of God's stars.

That particular day Mitch was wearing his blue home-spun shirt Sassafrass had made with laced cuffs, and an orange coral medallion and some copper corduroy pants that sat on his thighs like he was the hottest thing in town. But this time Mitch was serious and brusque when he spoke to Sassafrass, who was trying to push her crocheting under her skirts.

"Why aren't you writing, girl? Do you think you gonna be some kind of writer sitting up here making me hats? I got so many damn hats I have to give some away, and you sittin' here makin' me another one. Well, if I didn't know you were being so considerate because you don't wanna deal with your writing, I'd say thanks, but you makin' me stuff and hangin' all this shit around the walls in every room so you won't haveta write nothing today."

Sassafrass was holding her lips so tight between her teeth she could barely stand the pain, and she was making moves to get up and away from Mitch's harangue when he pushed her back on the bed.

"Look, Sassafrass, I just want you to be happy with yourself. You want to write and create new images for black folks, and you're always sittin' around making things with your hands. There's nothing wrong with that, 'cept you've known how to do that all your damn life." Mitch began to grow fierce again, and held Sassafrass briskly by the shoulder with one hand, bringing her chin and eyes straight to his gaze with the other. And Sassafrass couldn't avoid the truth: the man she loved was not happy with her charade of homebodiness, because all this weaving and crocheting and macrameing she'd been doing all her life, and Sassafrass was supposed to be a writer. Mitch forcefully held her face close to his and continued.

"Now Sassafrass, get into yourself and find out what's holding you back. You can create whole worlds, girl. I don't wanna come and see you like this any more, listening to some white man make it easy for you to stop thinking, telling you all the white folks' news, so you think that nobody doesn't know you got to pay your dues to the spirits. Sassafrass, if another person don't tell you you're a writer, you'll know it all your life. And you better take care of it or you'll end up some kind of wino or slut, trying to fuck it away with some punk-assed schoolteacher who can't see you a jive-assed little bitch." Mitch slowly let Sassafrass' face come into her control, and stood all the way up so Sassafrass couldn't forget who was overwhelmingly right in any situation. He straightened his shirt in his pants, and left the room to go practice horn playing.

Sassafrass was weak from Mitch's torrent. She sat so still her old fear of actually being a catatonic came back, and scared her so much she wiggled just to make sure. Mitch didn't have to say all that even if it was true; it was ridiculous for some man to come tell her she had to create. That's the same as telling her she had to have babies, and she didn't want to have babies . . . she could hardly feed herself, and Mitch didn't feed anybody. All he did was play that old horn, and look for the nearest bar that could use an "avant-garde free-music" sax man. "Humph." Sassafrass caught herself focusing in on Mitch again instead of herself, because she did want to be perfected for him, like he was perfected and creating all the time. Sassafrass was running all through herself looking for some way to get into her secrets and share, like Richard Wright had done and Zora Neale Hurston had done . . . the way The Lady gave herself, every time she sang.

Do Nothing till You Hear from Me
Pay No Attention to What's Said

From out of the closet came Billie, The Lady, all decked out in navy crêpe and rhinestones. She was pinning a gardenia in her hair, when Sassafrass realized what was happening.

The Lady sighed a familiar sigh. Sassafrass tried to look as calm as possible and said, "I sure am glad to see you—why you haven't come to visit since Mama used to put me to bed singing 'God Bless The Child,' and you would sit right on my pillow singing with her." The Lady smiled sort of haughty and insisted Sassafrass listen carefully to everything she was going to say.

*"It's the blues, Sassafrass, that's keepin' you from
your writing, and the spirits sent me because I know all
about the blues . . . that's who I am: Miss Brown's Blues
. . ."* The Lady was holding a pearl-studded cigarette
holder that dazzled Sassafrass, who could hardly believe
what she was hearing. The Lady went on and on. *"Who
do you love among us, Sassafrass? Ma Rainey, Mamie
Smith, Big Mama Thornton, Freddie Washington, Josephine, Carmen Miranda? Don't ya know we is all sad
ladies because we got the blues, and joyful women because we got our songs? Make you a song, Sassafrass,
and bring it out so high all us spirits can hold it and
be in your tune. We need you, Sassafrass, we need you
to sing best as you can; that's our nourishment, that's
how we live. But don't you get all high and mighty,
'cause all us you love so much is hussies too, and we
catch on if somebody don't do us right. So make us some
poems and some stories, so we can sing a liberation song.
Free us from all these blues and sorry ways."*

The Lady turned to the doorway on her right and
shouted, *"Come on, y'all,"* and multitudes of brown-
skinned dancing girls with ostrich-feather headpieces
and tap shoes started doing the cake-walk all around
Sassafrass, who was trying to figure out the stitching
pattern on their embroidered dresses, and trying to keep
from jumping up and shaking her ass when, in unison,
the elaborately beaded women started swinging their
hips toward her, singing: *SASSAFRASS IS WHERE
IT'S AT, SASSAFRASS GOTTA HIPFUL OF LOVE, A
HIPFUL OF TRUTH . . . SASSAFRASS GOTTA JOB
TO DO, DUES TO PAY SO SHE COULD DANCE
WITH US . . . WHOOEEE!*

And all of a sudden the chorus line disintegrated into
a dressing-room conversation; the women started sharing
secrets about lovers, managers, and children staying

*with their grandmas till the tour was over . . . and
Sassafrass gathered all there was that was more to her
than making cloth. Just as she was about to slip out of
the room, Sassafrass turned to The Lady to capture just
a little more of the magic, and The Lady only murmured, "We need you to be Sassafrass 'til you can't
hardly stand it . . . 'til you can't recognize yourself, and
you sing all the time."*

Sassafrass closed the door on the babbling women-
visitors quickly. Mitch was coming toward her, making
the room reel with the craziness of his music; like he was
tearing himself all up, beating and scratching through
his skin. The horn rocked gently with his body, but the
sounds were devastating: pure anger and revenge. He
pulled the slight instrument from his mouth and licked
the reed once or twice, before he slipped his hand up
Sassafrass' skirts to tickle her a little.

"You gonna make me something to eat, lovely one?"
Mitch grinned a Valentino grin, horn in one hand, Sassafrass on the other. She giggled distractedly and mumbled, "Yeah, I just wanna write down a few things before
I get stuck in the kitchen."

She rubbed her temples impatiently, because for a
change Mitch wasn't on her mind. She didn't want to
play; she wanted to write, and Mitch was messing
around, being nasty. She caught his wrist with her
thumb and index finger. "Not now, Mitch. Not now. I
wanna go do something." Mitch released her instantly.
He wasn't into taking any woman who didn't want him
desperately, so Sassafrass could go. And Mitch picked
up his horn and tooted the melody of Looney Tune
cartoons he had to watch when he was a child at the
boys' reformatory in Philadelphia: dadadadada dadadadada, and then he imitated Porky Pig saying, "t-t-t-t-
that's all, folks!" He smiled to himself when Sassafrass

slammed the door to the kitchen and made obviously rebellious noises with every pot she handled.

Mitch had convinced Sassafrass that everything was an art, so nothing in life could be approached lightly. Creation was inherent in everything anybody ever did right; that was one of the mottos of the house. Sassafrass had made an appliquéd banner saying just that, and hung it over the stove:

CREATION IS

EVERYTHING YOU DO

MAKE SOMETHING

She sat on her personal chair to concentrate on what to create for dinner. She was busy thinking of nothing when she fixed on the idea of a rice casserole, sautéed spinach and mushrooms with sweet peppers, and broiled mackerel with red sauce. If she prepared this scrumptious meal there wouldn't be hardly enough food left to finish off the week, but since Mitch was into her being perfect today, she decided to make a perfect meal and let him perfect out the menu for later, because "you can't cut no corners and be right" is what he always said. And Sassafrass set to work.

Sassafrass' Rice Casserole #36

1½ cups medium grain brown rice
3 ounces pimentos
1 cup baby green peas
½ cup fresh walnuts

⅔ pound smoked cheddar cheese
½ cup condensed milk
Diced garlic to taste
Cayenne to taste

Cook rice as usual. In an eight-inch baking dish, layer rice, cheese, pimentos, walnuts, and peas. Spread garlic and cayenne as you see fit. Pour milk around side of dish so it cushions rice against the edge. Bake in oven 20–30 minutes or until all the cheese melts and the top layer has a nice brown tinge.

Sassafrass' Favorite Spinach for Mitch #10

1–2 bunches Japanese
  spinach
8 good-sized mushrooms
2 tablespoons vegetable oil
  (safflower oil is very light)

2 tablespoons tamari
½ teaspoon finely crushed
  rosemary
4 sweet hot peppers

Wash spinach carefully in cold water. Break leaves from stem with fingers—do not cut—and set spinach in colander. Wash mushrooms. Slice vertically so each slice maintains its shape. Put oil in heavy iron skillet, heat until drop of water makes it pop. Turn flame down and lay spinach evenly in pan. Spread mushrooms; sprinkle rosemary and tamari. Simmer until leaves are soft and hot. Do not overcook. Place peppers in nice design around spinach and serve quickly.

Sassafrass: The Only Way to Broil Fish: Mackerel

Clean fish thoroughly. Dip in melted butter, add salt and pepper. Cook 4–6 minutes on each side in broiler.

Red Sauce: Sassafrass' Variation Du-Wop '59

1 small can tomato sauce
1 cup cooking sherry or
  sangria
½ cup finely chopped
  parsley

½ cup finely chopped onion
Garlic to taste
Cayenne

Mix tomato sauce and wine in saucepan. Add sautéed onions, parsley, and seasonings. Spread some sauce over fish while broiling; save the rest to use on plate.

While Sassafrass cooked she usually did yoga breathing exercises or belly dance pelvic contractions as she puttered around. The movements were almost accidental: tearing the spinach she'd contract on each pull from a stem and release as soon as it hit the colander. She would breathe ten quick breaths out and ten quick ones in as she crossed the kitchen from the sink to the stove. Not wanting to waste a moment, she would do *relevés* on alternate sets of ten contractions, so it would be: contract-*relevé*-release-down. This went on for as long as it took to cook dinner, and as the mackerel came out of the oven, Sassafrass was a buoyant and contented woman.

Sassafrass made her way out of the kitchen to get Mitch for dinner. She stepped into the studio to see how his art supplies were standing up against his create-every-day saga. The acrylic paints would probably last just another week before Mitch would have only ochre left; watercolors, sufficient; oils, absolutely tubes' end. Sassafrass was figuring the actual cost or barter price some new brushes would come to, when she heard calamitous booted feet traipsing through her house, and some men's voices upsetting her resting plants. She hurriedly took an overall inventory of Mitch's drawing equipment, and copped a gracious hostess attitude for the unexpected dinner guests. Otis and Howard Goodwin-Smith, two brothers from Chicago, had been in L.A. since Korea, most of their growing-up days. They tried, sometimes, to act like they were from Chi-town, but in a couple of minutes that Southern California hip-less-ness would ooze from every word. Otis was a writer, which made Sassafrass uneasy, and Howard was a painter of contorted phallic symbols dipped in Afrikan mystique and loaded with latent rapist bravado. The Goodwin-Smiths from the South Side. Sassafrass held her tongue while she greeted them; she wanted to ask why they hadn't brought their white wives. She felt her eyes sneer and her mouth smile, saying, "Too bad Jennie and Olga couldn't make it . . . I never see them, you know."

Otis and Howard looked over to Mitch, who was looking at Albert the dog, to make sure Sassafrass could enjoy putting the brothers on the spot. Then Albert moved over to Howard, who was kneeling on the floor trying to get a whole idea of Mitch's new mural. Albert on his haunches was almost six feet, and he got on his haunches to try to hump the chauvinist Howard. Sassafrass saw Albert rear back and slam his front paws across Howard's back, saw his dick hanging oily-like from its fur pouch, aiming for Howard's jeans-covered backside. Howard was shocked, and steady trying to get out of Albert's way. They made circles around the room, Albert chasing Howard past the aging velvet couch, the barber's seat that doubled as a chaise longue, the driftwood coffee table, and the mural lying on the floor. Round and round they went. Sassafrass glimmered, and went to get the food. Mitch started playing the Lone Ranger's theme song. Otis was rolled over laughing, and Howard finally tore off one of his sneakers to appease Albert, who always tried to make it with small men. They ate with chopsticks, in time to Ron Carter's *Uptown Conversation*.

Otis had reconnoitered the barber's seat for himself, and from his lofty perch, began, "I brought y'all a copy of my new book, *Ebony Cunt* . . . I autographed it special, Mitch; see here . . ."

> *for sassafrass . . .*
> *I know yours is good*

Sassafrass' face nearly hit the floor. She glanced at Mitch to see where he was at, and he was enjoying his clout with the fellas, because he announced: "Sassafrass got some of the best pussy west of the Rockies, man, and I don't care who knows it, 'cause it's mine!"

They all laughed raucously, except Sassafrass was glaring from her inmost marrow and wishing there was some way to get rid of male crassness once and for all time. She called herself being kind to Mitch, because he liked his friends, while she began discreetly leaving the room. But Otis called out for a thorough reading of his new work, to Mitch's accompaniment on sax and Howard's innovative percussion with a worndown tambourine.

THE REVUE

Otis
Sassafrass, you gotta sit in this barber chair and be the queen you are, while I read this masterpiece *(teehee)* of mine for all y'all black women all over the world.

Sassafrass
Otis, I, ah, gotta get started on something, ya know.

Otis, Mitch, Howard (in unison)
Nononono . . . you gotta hear this one, babeee!

(Mitch picks Sassafrass off her feet and places her in the chair, squeezes her leg, and smiles)

Mitch
Go on, Otis. We gotta celebrate this woman of mine even if she doesn't understand why we gotta have her, every morning . . . in the evenin' when the sun go down . . .

87/

*(Mitch sings like he is Ray Charles, and shakes all
around like Little Richard)*

Otis

I'ma start now. I'ma read all about it, but first I wanna
say, a la Edwin Starr circa 1963:

> *extra extra reeeeeeead allll about itttttt*
> *extra extra reeeeeeead allll about itttttt*

*(Howard, Mitch, and Otis do old Temptations Apollo
routines around Sassafrass, who is enjoying this worship
from the du-wop straddlers in spite of herself)*

Howard

Aw right. Now Otis, get it on . . . we ready.

Otis

EBONY CUNT: for my mama and my grandma and all the
women I rammed in Macon, Georgia when I was visitin'
my cousins at age sixteen:

The white man want you/ the Indian run off with
you
Spaniards created whole nations with you/ black
queensilk snatch
I wander all in your wombs & make babies in the
Bronx when I come/ you screammmmmmm/ jesus/
my blk man
ebony cunt is worth all the gold in the world/ 15
millions of your shinin' blk bodies crossed the sea
to bring all that good slick pussy to me . . .

*(Sassafrass stands up like a mannequin, and gazes abso-
lutely redfaced at Otis, Mitch, and Howard, all of whom
stare back at her, uncomprehending)*

Mitch
Sassafrass, what's wrong with you? Sit down. Otis gotta finish the book; he isn't even done with the first page . . .

Sassafrass (standing still)
Just one god-damned minute, Mitch. You gotta mother you supposedly love so much, and a daughter by a black woman who won't see you . . . and you got me all messed up, and tryin' to make you happy . . . god damn it, I don't haveta listen to this shit. I am not interested in your sick, sick, weakly rhapsodies about all the women you fucked in all your damn lives . . . I don't like it. I am not about to sit heah and listen to a bunch of no account niggahs talk about black women; me and my sisters; like we was the same bought and sold at slave auction . . . breeding heifers the white man created 'cause y'all was fascinated by some god damn beads he brought you on the continent . . . muthafuckahs. Yeah, that's right; muthafuckahs, don't you ever sit in my house and ask me to celebrate my inherited right to be raped. Goddamn muthafuckahs. Don't you know about anythin' besides taking women off, or is that really all you good for?

(Mitch looks at Sassafrass like she was a harlot. He puts his horn away and remains silent. Otis and Howard chuckle nervously, and get ready to split)

Otis
Look now Sassafrass, I'm sorry you took it the wrong way . . .

(He smiles. All three men leave the house. On the way out, Howard pokes his head back through the bagging-screen door)

Howard
I don't care *what* you say, Sassafrass . . . I *know* you got
good pussy!

*(They all laugh jauntily on the way to the '59 Chevy
2-door sedan. Sassafrass stands still in front of the barber's chair for an indefinite time)*

When she moved, she went to her looms . . .

> *makin cloth, bein a woman & longin*
> *to be of the earth*
> *a rooted blues*
> *some ripe berries*
> *happenin inside*
> *spirits*
> *walkin in a dirt road*
> *toes dusted & free*
> *faces movin windy*
> *brisk like*
> *dawn round*
> *gingham windows &*
> *opened eyes*
> *reelin to days*
> *ready-made*
> *nature's image*
> *i'm rejoicin*
> *with a throat deep*
> *shout & slow*
> *like a river*
> *gatherin*
> *space*

*i am sassafrass/ a weaver's daughter/ from
charleston/ i'm a woman makin cloth like all good
women do/ the moon's daughter made cloth/ the
gold array of the sun/ the moon's daughter sat all
night/ spinnin/ i have inherited fingers that change
fleece to tender garments/ i am the maker of warmth
& emblems of good spirit/ mama/ didn't ya show me
how/ to warp a loom/ to pattern stars into cotton
homespun/ mama/ didn't ya name me for yr favorite
natural dye/ sassafrass/ so strong & even/ go good
with deep fertile greens/ & make tea to temper chilly
evenings/ i'm a weaver with my sistahs from any
earth & fields/ we always make cloth/ love our
children/ honor our men/ who protect us from our
enemies/ we prepare altars & anoint candles to offer
our devotion to our guardians/ we proffer hope/ &
food to eat/ clothes to wear/ wombs to fill.*

Almost unconsciously Sassafrass had begun the labo-
rious process of warping the four-harness table loom she
had transported from Charleston. The eccentric family
her family had worked for as slaves, and then as freed
women weavers, had seen fit to grant Sassafrass the
looms her forebears had warped and wefted thousands
of times since emancipation. Sassafrass had always been
proud that her mother had a craft; that all the women
in her family could make something besides a baby, and
shooting streams of sperm. She had grown up in a room
full of spinning wheels, table and floor looms, and her
mother always busy making cloth because the Fitzhugh
family never wore anything but hand-woven cloth . . .
until they couldn't afford it any more. Sassafrass had
never wanted to weave, she just couldn't help it. There
was something about the feel of raw fleece and finished
threads and dainty patterned pieces that was as essential

to her as dancing is to Carmen DeLavallade, or singing
to Aretha Franklin. Her mama had done it, and her
mama before that; and making cloth was the only tradi-
tion Sassafrass inherited that gave her a sense of womanhood that was rich and sensuous, not tired and stingy.
She thought that if Kingfish had bought Sapphire a
loom, she would never have been such a bitch. She
thought that the bronze Dionysius was not saving the sad
frigid women of Thebes by seducing them away from
their looms, but rather he was planning, under Osiris'
aegis, to wipe out Europeans before they went around
the world enslaving rainbow-colored people . . . because
when women make cloth, they have time to think, and
Theban women stopped thinking, and the town fell. So
Sassafrass was certain of the necessity of her skill for the
well-being of women everywhere, as well as for her own.
As she passed the shuttle through the claret cotton warp,
Sassafrass conjured images of women weaving from all
time and all places: Toltecas spinning shimmering
threads; East Indian women designing intricate patterns
for Shakti, the impetus and destruction of creation; and
Navajo women working on thick tapestries. She tried to
compel an African woman to come join them—women,
making cloth—and the spirits said, "No. You cannot
have her . . . in Africa men make cloth, and women
. . ." Sassafrass tossed her head to the left side, and
dismissed her congregation of international cloth mak-
ers while she rethreaded her shuttle. And Mitch was
home . . .

Hi there Sassafrass . . .

How's mama's favorite dumpling? Sounds to me like you have indeed worked wonders on your little house. Just watch now that you don't overdo with too much color. Houses are supposed to comfort us, as well as invigorate the senses. You don't get one by ignoring the other. There, you see, I do have a notion of aesthetics, black or not. They're Southern, and that's close enough. (smile)

The Wheeler girls came home from Vassar last week. They were a little behind you, I think. At any rate, they have gone completely African. Changed their names; wear these big old pieces of cloth . . . look just like mammies, to my mind. Their mother, Gertie, has refused to let them out of the house till they go round to Mrs. Calhoun's and get that hair pressed. So, it's all right that you and your sisters don't come home, when I think about how you must look!

That little Schuyler boy, the one who went to Dartmouth and is now at Meharry, has wrecked two cars already, and still his father hasn't put his foot down. I can't understand loving somebody so much, you let them make you a fool, but, thank god he's no child of mine. That's that boy who *kept you out all weekend when I came to visit you in New England. Don't try to act like I'm mistaken—I may not be a liberated woman, but I wasn't born yesterday. I can't see what you saw in him. For all that breeding, and the money spent on him, he acts like a natural-born hoodlum.*

What else . . . oh, guess what? Your name is in the alumni magazine of the Callahan School. Seems like you are the only one, out of all those rich children, to go on ahead and be an artist. Don't be upset with me. I sent the information in myself, with samples of your work. It's the least I could do, after Mrs. Fitzhugh sponsored you and all. I can't understand why you hated that place so . . . not going to your graduation, refusing to go on to college. Oh, Sassafrass, weaving is a fine craft, but with the opportunities open to Negroes your age, I just don't know why you insist on doing everything the hard way.

I hate to say this, but it follows my thoughts about your resisting the bounties our Lord has laid before you, in order to take up with the most unfortunate among us. How could you take up with a man who wasn't raised in a proper home . . . not even an orphan, just a delinquent? Even I have heard stories of the terrible conditions in the reform schools, and here my very own daughter searches far and wide, moves all the way to California, to fall in love with a man who has nothing to offer, no background, no education, no future. If you think for a minute, darling, you'll see that all the training you've had is far and away more than that boy can imagine. So what is it that you're going to learn from him? You should get down on your knees and pray for guidance. And while you're down there, thank the Lord for giving you the good sense not to compromise yourself by living in sin. You can at least still meet some more folks who are up to you, and who'll appreciate what a fine young woman you are. Truly, dear, try to get out and enjoy yourself. The race has had problems ever since we got here.

You can't do anything about them by staying in your house, refusing to take part in the world you belong in.

Call cousin Loreen. I told you, her step-sons are all doctors, and mighty good-looking . . . (a word to the wise).

Love,
Mama

P.S. You don't have to tell Mitch everything I said about him . . . if that's an open relationship, humpf. You need a closed one!!

L. A. nights are not quite dark; the lights from all the freeways keep it in a zone of perpetual twilight, so Sassafrass rarely used electric lights, only candles. As she peeked from her weaving room to see where Mitch was playing his horn, the house, her house, was a blueberry-tinged house. She thought the furniture and paintings lining the walls were enveloped in a blueberry aura, and that comforted her, seeking Mitch.

"Hey Sassafrass, come catch this action!"

Mitch was in the front room. Sassafrass hadn't approached that room by fifteen feet since Howard and Otis had left. She timorously made her way through the icy blue haunts of her realms to see what new trip Mitch had fixed on this time. She was even charmed by the idea he had called for her so soon; soon as he came in. Mitch was grinning with his horn in one hand, and a strange, accordian-shaped tube in the other.

"Hey there, beloved," Sassafrass slurred coquettishly, "what's up?" Mitch was magnificent in an orange crêpe jacket with beaded eagles; Quetzal, the Aztecs' creativity spirit, flying across his breast, and the Ashanti-styled bead choker Sassafrass had arduously finished for him only days ago. Mitch was grinning and magnificent, but he didn't respond to Sassafrass; he started walking back and forth in front of her, without taking his eyes off her. He was grinning and quiet, and with all the force he had and all his exquisite grace, he struck her across the face with the tube. Then he laughed out loud, and moved the tube to his mouth; made deep wispy sounds like beer-bottle tooters, then he hit her again, still laughing.

Sassafrass was stunned. She did not move, she didn't speak. Mitch tossed the tube in the air and it curled up like the toy snakes kids have at circuses; Sassafrass ran to pick it up, and Mitch shoved her to the side. Once he had the tube in his hands again, he twirled it—and he struck again, again, and again.

"Mitch, have you gone crazy . . . stop, stop, stop . . . I can't stand it, you're hurting me . . . stop it, Mitch, you are hurtin' me!" And he stopped, picked up his horn, and began to play the solo from Eric Dolphy's *Green Dolphin Street* cut. Sassafrass left the room slowly, bewildered and frantic. And Mitch said nothing.

Sassafrass wandered hesitantly through the kitchen. In vague ways she picked up the car keys, let the dog out, and changed the Kitty Litter. She locked the door to the weaving room, and eventually left the house. She sat in the car in front of the house for at least an hour. She had never been beaten by a man; she had sworn that whoever did, she would leave. And she had told Mitch, in the Japanese garden in Exposition Park when they had first met, "If you ever strike me, I will leave you or see you in jail." Mitch hadn't said anything then, just as he didn't say anything tonight. And Sassafrass cried, tormented, and afraid she would have to leave Mitch, whom she adored. She started the tumbling-down auto and drove from the Pasadena Freeway to Santa Monica, where she stopped to watch the sun rise over the deserted beach. Sassafrass was locked, like all the barred and dingy wharf cafeterias. She was tight, and the ocean nibbling her ankles in another dawn did not arouse her spirit. Instead, the monotonous coming back, coming back of the waves reminded her that she, too, would return to her own rubble-strewn shores. She was going to go back to Mitch; she could not leave . . . not now. Sassafrass was afraid to look at the sun for fear the golden garments the moon's daughter had woven would rot from her gaze. She had betrayed trust and prophesied inviolate independence. She was a woman, and she was strong—and she loved Mitch; had only served as an instrument for the will of the spirits. She'd been too headstrong, too sure she needed no man; and she did understand, now, that she needed Mitch of all things in the world. She needed Mitch because Mitch was all she loved in herself.

It wasn't so far from what she remembered . . . that night it had rained something terrible in Charleston, rained so hard she and Cypress put Indigo at the foot of the bed under the covers with them, in case all the trees round the house came crashing through the roof—like they were bound to, since they were shaking and scratching and making awful noises that left children speechless and quaking. The other noises were her mama and daddy shouting; mixing in with the howling wind till the commotion on the stairs forced all the girls to creep to the door, because it wasn't just the hurricane that was upsetting everything.

"Daddy, let go a mama! Daddy let go!" That's all she shouted, as she watched her mama being pulled down the stairs toward the front door, her hair in the grip of

*his fists. It was raining, and the girls were all crying so
. . . their mother looked so tiny in her nightgown and
bare feet, battered by the rain on the front porch. There
were more screaming noises between the adults, along
with the whimpers of the girls, the thrashings of the
forsythia 'gainst the screens . . . but when it was all over,
and the girls had vowed never to speak to their father
again on account of his hurting their mother, all Mama
had said was, "You got to leave room for the fool in
everybody."*

By the time Sassafrass got back to Highland Park it
was late morning. She had insisted to herself that getting
caught in the early rush hour was just another debt she
had to pay for being a brazen hussy, and she pulled the
front door of her house vigorously because she knew
more of what she wanted in this life, and Mitch was most
of it . . . and he was in there waiting for her. The queer
silence puzzled her; usually Mitch would be practicing,
or humming to himself while he painted. Sassafrass felt
a knot in her heart. She went through each room with
more anxiety—in the kitchen Mitch sat nodding out, by
the window. She ran to the bathroom . . . blood. Blood
was on the bathroom floor again; Mitch's junkie works
were lingering on the sink. And Sassafrass let whole
worlds, dreams, and kisses, fall from her eyes. Deftly,
almost mechanically, she cleaned up the mess Mitch and
some of his friends must have made. She fed the animals, straightened each room, and finally went to where
Mitch was sitting, sleeping. She stroked his cheek with
her hand; she loved him. She kissed him on temples, on
cheeks—each one—and then she kissed his lips ten-
derly and long. He woke up a little. Sassafrass kissed
him again, and one more time he responded. When he
was relatively lucid, in the middle of touching his eye-

brow with her full mouth, she whispered, "You're a lousy, stinkin' junkie, Mitch. I haveta go now."

She packed two large bags: one filled with clothes, the other with notebooks and yarns and needles of all sorts. She left some money with Cleo, the neighbor, to buy food for Albert and the cat they kept, and told Cleo to tell Mitch she would send for her things. She left on a 3:00 shuttle flight to San Francisco, to stay with her sister Cypress. In the airports, on the buses, Sassafrass kept saying, "He never promised me anything . . . I didn't ask for a ring, no money, no monogamy . . . just no dope." She made no attempt to smile, once she got to Cypress' house. She was of the same stone as Isis, searching for the lost Osiris. She drank some black Guatemalan coffee, and stalked off to the room Cypress saved for her to begin another piece of cloth.

ypress was always smiling. She had made
amends with her living, and thoroughly expected everything to happen to her, given time and the way her luck
ran. She was round and sturdy, but elastic like a gather-
ing of sunflowers in a balmy night. Cypress liked sweet
wine, cocaine, and lots of men: musicians, painters,
poets, sculptors . . . photographers, filmmakers, airplane
pilots. Her house was full of folks from dusk to noon;
and she was usually draped in an oriental robe glossed
with coffee stains and the smell of her body. Sassafrass'
arrival didn't disrupt the hoopla that was Cypress' home,
because Cypress had, in her easy, cynical way, told every
soul she knew that her sister would be coming soon.
Cypress was sure that no real man could put up with
Sassafrass' absolute demands for total involvement, total
perfection, total personhood for more than two or three
months. Cypress was sure that when a man knew his
woman knew he wasn't near perfect, or going to be, one
of them would have to split. So she held on to a room
for Sassafrass, and chuckled about the closed door and
glum face Sassafrass used as protection from the many
possible suitors lingering around.

Cypress' kitchen was deep amber, and the rest of the rooms were all swamp green. She didn't allow any chairs in her house, only pillows—and no shoes, either. She insisted on respect for her space, and was liable to throw out visitors who didn't follow the rules:

WHEN YOU STEP THROUGH THIS DOOR/
YOU'RE IN MY HOUSE

1. *Wash all dishes you use & put them back*
2. *Empty ashtrays when full*
3. *Change beds every two days*
4. *Don't leave any clothes lying around*
5. *Don't use any profane language*
6. *Don't talk loudly*
7. *Don't bring any dope fiends around here*
8. *Don't touch the altar for the Orishas*
9. *Don't take anything for granted*

MAY THE SPIRITS BLESS YOU

Sassafrass didn't really know anybody but Cypress in San Francisco, and she was cold all the time. Her thin smocks for L.A.'s perpetual spring didn't have the stuff in them to cope with the dense fog and chill of northern California; the cold she felt continually reminded her that she was alone—forsaken, she liked to believe. She huddled in her room with her mama's carders (Cypress had dug them out of some ancient trunk), and prepared fleece for spinning. She would hum spirituals to herself, like "His Eye Is on the Sparrow, and I Know He's Watchin' Me" or "Jesus Is Just Awright with Me, Jesus Is Just Awright with Me" and "I Come to the Garden Alone." Leroy McCullough would stand in front of her door and sing be-bop love messages to her: "Sassafrass gotta mighty fine ass; won't you come and play with me . . . be-blee-de—oh-wha-doo . . ." And Cypress would matter-of-factly respond, "Sassafrass is busy today, can you call again tomorrow." And then whoever was there would just laugh, or toot a horn. Sassafrass would sing her old time praises of the Lord louder, until everyone got quiet, and she shushed too, eventually, and maybe cried or sat among all her wools and stared at the fading floral-pattern floor.

Cypress' house smelled like curry, and when she wasn't cooking, she was dancing down at the studio with most of the folks she was cooking for. There was something about dancing that was family, and Cypress loved her family. She could definitely put herself out for some dancer-honkytonk-singer friend in a second, but she could definitely put herself on some railroad tracks for her blood sister. At least that's how Cypress got herself around to cornering Sassafrass about her "melancholia."

Sassafrass was trying to be busy, winding thread and counting warp ends per inch, when Cypress caught some of the orange cotton between her toes, in a perfectly executed *grande battement.* Sassafrass looked piqued, and meowed, "Cypress, you know as well as I do, you've always been too bouffant to be any kind of dancer, get your ducky leg outta my yarn. Please, dear." Cypress was twenty years used to remarks about her peasant figure, and didn't give two hoots, so she let Sassafrass wrestle with the uselessness of sibling slurs and began packing the stray threads away, like any weaver's daughter would. She called on all the hopefulness in her core to get Sassafrass to let loose a little and feel the newness of where she was really at. Cypress just moved through Sassafrass' supplies like she was Sassafrass' shadow, and Sassafrass watched her sister being impeccable as usual, and realized this was one of those times Cypress would have her way. So she allowed Cypress to lead her by the hand into the kitchen, same as they used to go sneak coffee way into the night at Mama's, so many questions past.

Sassafrass languidly positioned herself in a paunchy straw mat, waiting for Cypress' inevitable "sermon for the daughter of little faith." She smiled inconspicuously as Cypress almost glided back and forth across the room. "She really is elegant," Sassafrass thought, as she attended to the womanly grace oozing out of Cypress' every motion.

"Well, Cypress, what's on the corner of your fat ol' ass?" Sassafrass could hardly believe herself, but she kept on. "Now Cypress, I want you to tell me all about my future, and how bright the sun's going to be shining in my back door some day."

Sassafrass was wheeling in her seat as though she was showering in scotch whiskey. "Did you hear, Cypress? I wanna know all about how I got it made, and ain't got no cause to be gloomy right now."

Cypress just giggled, and placed some cream cheese and pineapple concoctions on the table next to a fresh porcelain pot of coffee. She slid into a seat exactly opposite Sassafrass and murmured, "Why don't you let me know what all went down with Mitch, because I ain't got a thing to say 'til I know if you're still a devoted mistress."

Sassafrass blushed and threw her arms in the air like she was going to choke flies . . . then she saw Cypress' face held no malice, no judgment. Cypress nestled her head up against the side of the stove, and started again.

"Sassafrass, isn't there anything you can say about

what happened between you and Mitch . . . or is that
top-secret-confidential he-ro-in' just between you and
him?"

Sassafrass pulled her chin up and out, like a prouder
woman than she was, and sucked in her teeth like she
was thinking what a bore this all was. Cypress delighted
in her canapés and coffee, until she decided playtime
was over.

"Look-a-heah, Sassafrass, Miz Been-Thru-It-All. I
need to talk to you. I know better than you how hard it
is to live with an artist . . . the 'artiste.' Black men ain't
no easy picking; ain't no easy staying. That's why I keep
them all coming here, then I don't have to pick not a one,
and can keep them all. But you aren't like me, Sassafrass. You got to have you a single cosmic wonder with
more than all the troubles of Hades in his horns and
arms. Come on, girl. Will you tell me what's going on?
'Sides, I might want to rent that room, if you're going
back to him."

Cypress' astounding request set Sassafrass to laughing, and finally able to share the events of her last few
days with Mitch, she poured out anecdote after anecdote,
telling Cypress all his good points and all his weak-
nesses.

"Ses faiblesses," Cypress cynicized, "gonna cost you
all the hair on your head and probably any joy you were
expecting."

Sassafrass stuck by her man whom she had abandoned, and became healthily articulate about her problem. "Now Cypress, Mitch has endured more loneliness
than a human being should ever encounter. His mother
abandoned him when he was eight, and he raised himself in detention homes all thru this country full of
crackers and madmen. Mitch is so good—he created
himself; he made up somebody to be. Inside the joint,

he took up horn playing and painting. Mitch is so strong, Cypress—he just gets that loneliness sometimes . . ."

Sassafrass waited on that word "loneliness" for a sign of understanding from Cypress, who was staring right through her. Cypress was rendering all her lovers past, who could leap with the fire of Shango racing through their limbs, and make her cry from the beauty of their incarnate spirits. Cypress remembered every torrid affair —like a *Hit Parade* from the fifties. She was close to a primal scream, when Sassafrass interrupted.

"I left, Cypress, 'cause Mitch broke the only promise he ever made to me. That's all a matter of trust, that's all . . . he didn't keep his word. 'Cause I don't want to marry anybody—have them own half of all Mama's stuff, and half of all my stuff, and claim visiting rights for my kids and money and all that mess—I couldn't stand it. So I'm all right pretending to be kept while I keep up my share, but I can't abide breaking promises. Honest, Cypress, that's all."

Cypress was exercising her arches and her toes, pushing through the calf and heel to the ball of her foot to point, then flex. Point; flex. She heard Sassafrass and nodded her head, concentrating on her form . . . then she was back.

"Well, Sassafrass, what're you gonna do?"

Sassafrass was charmed by her sister's dedication and bluntness. "I'm gonna stay here and go to dance with you and show you my new weaving techniques. And I'm gonna write, Cypress. I'm gonna write about Mama, and growing up with all those looms."

Cypress smiled so wide, like her hips, and the two of them gobbled up some more cottage cheese right out of the box. They began picking up their dirtied dishes and straightening out the kitchen; Cypress turned on the jazz FM station that was still into the apogee of be-bop, but was black, nonetheless, and the two of them offered themselves to the love they had for each other, improvising. Cypress would initiate a movement series and Sassafrass would respond; saucers in hand and crumbs circling their shoulders, they marked the "Sisters Cakewalk Jamboree—Delfonics style." Sassafrass disclosed her most secret desire to get to the artists' commune in Louisiana—the single alternative to Mitch's frustrations and her own. Cypress wasn't too overwhelmed by the prospect of spending time in the back bush of the South, but Cypress was a schemer too, and started finagling as soon as Sassafrass announced that all she and Mitch needed was about $800.00. Digging around in the drawer she kept all her Chinese cutlery in, Cypress grasped a thin compact with aqua rhinestones and pink-colored pearls. She opened it delicately, and her eyes just beamed. "You want a lil of this, Sassafrass?" Cypress generously held the compact of hoarded cocaine toward Sassafrass' chin. Sassafrass turned toward her sister, almost astonished at what she had known all along: Cypress was the "Coke Lady." Sassafrass pushed her chin back to her adam's apple, and shook her head. "Noooo thanks, loneliness." Cypress, with razor blade in one hand and straw in the other, had unwrapped a small piece of rice paper and was getting into her stuff. Sassafrass, who never paid much attention to time, suddenly noticed it was getting round the time to leave for the performance. Cypress had a two-hour rehearsal and then a show, and Sassafrass was going to help dress the women dancers in their elaborate costumes and fix anything looking like it might fall down in the middle of a running jump. Sassafrass got up out of her chair and started singing "Tonight's The Night," with all the Shirelles machinations: swivelling of hips and arms beckoning whatever lovers. Cypress could

hardly stand it, and said, "Come on, girl . . . we goin'
dancin'."

*down to the wharf, there was always sailors/ shippers
from all over the world/ daddy was a seaman/ a ship's
carpenter. he was always goin' round the world/ that's
what mama said/ & he died in the ocean offa
zanzibar/ that's what mama said the ship just caught
fire/ & went on down to the bottom of the ocean/ that's
why she & sassafrass & cypress & indigo/ wd toss
nickels & food & wine in the sea down the coast/ so
daddy wd have all he needed to live a good life in the
other world. sassafrass stayed by the wharf whenever she
cd/ after school she watched the men tyin knots/ fixin
nets & she figured her daddy knew all that/ & he cd
sing too like the sailors & dance like the west indians/
who was crew on a lotta boats in the seamy port of
charleston. sassafrass wd sit on barrels wid the men &
help 'em straighten out their nets/ & listen to the tales
of other colored folks' lives in the islands & as far off
as new guinea. she tried to imagine what they looked
like/ if they weren't tryin to look like white folks/ what
did the languages sound like/ & the cloth & the dance
& who were their spirits/ did they believe in jesus or
were there other gods/ & other heavens/ like there were
drums & special dances the bermudans & trinidadian
sailors played in the evenin/ & showed sassafrass what
they called the "jump-up"/ or the mambo/ sassafrass
picked up a slight accent/ & put her hand on her hip
the way the men did when they were imitatin' their
girls at home/ & sassafrass prayed she cd live like
that/ free in the country/ surrounded by orange trees &
men makin drums & goin out to fish & feasts for the
different spirits. sassafrass decided/
bein with the colored sailors & dock workers/ that she*

shd go everywhere there were dark folks at all/ all over
the world where her people lived/ & she wd write it all
down so other children wdnt feel lost & think they were
stupid ninnies/ like miz fitzhugh told her/ "it's too bad
you a lil ninny, sassafrass, or i'd take you with me on
this cruise"/ & to the surprise of the spry seafarers/
sassafrass announced/ "i'ma be a cunjah."
they laughed incredulously/ sayin/ "you awready a
geechee/ how much more magic you want?"
   sassafrass wished on flowers/ the flight patterns of
birds/ the angle of leaves fallin/ & swore to bring the
old ways back/ old spirits & their children & any
new-fandangled kinda mystic aids that was
demonstrated by circumstances. sassafrass stopped
hangin round by the wharf & started hangin round the
old folks at the church & bars in skinny streets/
learnin how to fix up sick folks/ & spells that so-&-so's
granny used ta murder whoever. & she layed up nights
readin' histories of ancient civilizations that were closer
to her than all that stuff abt england & the wars of the
roses.
she wrote songs of love & vindication for all the african
& indian deities disgraced by the comin of the white
man/ & loss of land/ & cities reflectin' respect for
livin' things.

   "i am sassafrass/ my fingers behold you
   i call upon you with my song you teach
   me in my sleep/ i am not a besieger of yr
   fortress/ i am a crusader/ for you are
   all my past/ i offer you my body to
   make manifest yr will in this dungeon
   of machines & carolina blues/ i wanna
   sing yr joy/ & make present our beauty/
   spirits/ black & brown/ find yr way

Ntozake Shange

> *thru my tainted blood/ make me one of*
> *yr own/ i am yr child in the new world/*
> *i am yr fruit/ yet to be chosen for*
> *a single battle in yr behalf/ come to*
> *& thru me/ i am dazzled by yr beneficence*
> *i shall create new altars/ new praises*
> *& be ancient among you/"*

Before reaching the door, Cypress opened up a large stained-glass box and pulled out four finely embroidered pieces of cloth.

"Hey, Miz Weaver . . . Sassafrass. These are my inheritances for some children I don't have yet."

Sassafrass looked over, and saw blocks of minute figures and arrows and circles in different colors. Cypress became terribly excited while she explained that each of the cloths was a complete notation of a dance developed from her own experiences in The Kushites Returned. Sassafrass checked that the stitches were even and the designs exceedingly intricate.

"Cypress, if the white folks knew you were doin' this, they'd steal all of it and put it in a museum!"

Cypress was wallowing in Sassafrass' appreciative statement when she recalled what their mama had said: "Whatever ideas you have that're important to you, write down . . . but write them so your enemies can't understand them right off." Feeling triumphant, Sassafrass and Cypress did the time step down Fulton Street.

At the bus stop, the two sisters enjoyed one more childhood pastime: singing rhythm and blues; first, Tina Turner's "I'm Just a Fool, You Know I'm in Love" and then the Marvelettes: *"I saida look, look, heah comes the postman, twistin' down the avenue . . . he's gotta lettah in his hand, an' I know it's gotta be from you-who*

110/

ooooooooo." And Cypress announced plans for a whoop-la get-down after the show at her house, with lots of good wine, and good, good food. Like maybe . . .

Three C's: Cypress' Curried Crabmeat

2 tablespoons vegetable oil
1 onion, chopped
1 fresh or canned green chili pepper, chopped (seed removed)
½ teaspoon grated ginger (¼ ground)
¼ teaspoon turmeric

Pinch of cinnamon
Pinch of ground cloves
Pinch ground cardamom
1½ cups cooked crabmeat
Salt
2 tablespoons chopped parsley
2 tablespoons lemon juice

Heat vegetable oil and fry the onion until soft. Add chili pepper and ginger, turmeric, cinnamon, cloves, and cardamom, and fry for 3 minutes, sprinkling with water to avoid burning. Add crabmeat and salt to taste. Stir and cook for 5 minutes. Sprinkle with lemon juice and chopped parsley. (serves 4)

My Mama & Her Mama 'Fore Her: Codfish Cakes (Accra)

4 ounces salt fish (cod)
2 cups flour
1 teaspoon dried yeast
2 blades chives, chopped

1 small onion, chopped
¼ teaspoon black pepper
1½ cups warm water
1 teaspoon sugar

Put yeast and sugar in bowl with ½ cup water, and set aside. Soak fish for ½ hour, remove skin and bone. Pound fish, chives, onion, and pepper until very fine. Sift flour with yeast mixture and add rest of water; stir until a soft batter is formed. Let stand in a warm place. Add fish mixture and beat for 2–3 minutes. Spoon fish into smoking oil. Drain, and serve with hot floats.

De Floats Be-fore de Fish

1 pound flour	1 teaspoon dried yeast
4 ounces shortening	1 teaspoon sugar
1½ teaspoons salt	Warm water

Mix yeast, sugar, and a little water in bowl and set aside for a few minutes. Sift flour and salt together; add shortening, yeast mixture, and enough water to make a soft dough. Knead until smooth. Put to rise in a warm place for 2 hours or until dough has doubled. Punch down. Knead again, cut dough into small pieces, and roll pieces into balls. Put to rise again for 20 minutes. Flatten balls out to ⅛-inch thickness and fry in smoking hot oil. Drain and serve hot.

Cypress' Sweetbread: The Goodness

Use any kind of cornmeal, add cooked beans and mashed sweet potatoes, baking soda, salt, a dash of cinnamon, and ¼ cup honey. Cook in pan as ordinary cornbread. Eat hot or cold.

Backstage, and the dressing rooms already smelled like sweat and sweet perfumes to mute incipient funk. Cypress just about shoved Sassafrass into Malik's arms trying to get to a table with a mirror; Sassafrass was feeling in the way, and decided to sit in a corner until the dancers were ready to get into costumes. Cypress sat down and proceeded to pile all different containers of stage makeup in front of her; she had to paint her face for the dress rehearsal, to see how a new design would look. When she finally finished, there wasn't a flesh-colored speck from her shoulders to her hairline. Cypress was the blue of prize Navajo turquoise, with yellow spirals racing down her cheeks; she was the Milky Way

at dawn. And Malik was painted scarlet with comets
flaring across his chest. Lallah and Melissa were passion-
flower orange with flame tips around their eyes; Eddie
and Guy were brazen sunlight yellow. In tights and
knitted leotards, everyone went through warm-ups on
the floor with Ariel, who insisted on wearing his se-
quined and satin cape for good luck with the spirits.
Stretches and lifts were mostly what Ariel had them
doing, and Cypress managed to ease over to Malik in the
back line, so she could discuss some business. In the
middle of the high kick series, Cypress stage-whispered,
"Malik, you got any corners on some blow?" Malik
smiled, but braced up real quick, because he had missed
a kick trying to listen to Cypress. Malik was one of those
thin dancing men, but without knobby bones sticking
out of every crook of his body. Malik was lithe like
nobody since the Step Brothers, and he was in love with
Cypress . . . as much as any dancer loves somebody
besides dance herself. Malik was puzzled by Cypress'
inquiry; she didn't ever buy any dope at all, she was just
around when somebody had some . . . or maybe she
wasn't. Cypress didn't yearn for any snow, and Malik
was very cool about his business off the dance floor. "I
don't now, Cypress; maybe. I'll let ya know." Meanwhile, Ariel had focused on the pair whispering in the
rear, and shouted clear across the room, like an unexpected blow-out.

"Malik. Cypress. Get those legs up. And keep your
hips front!" Cypress stopped thinking about anything
besides her body movement until after the performance.

BLACK OUT

The audience is seated and honeying up to itself.
Black men and women in miniskirts and wigs, dashikis
and flowing robes, rub tootsies and exchange greetings

through the dark. Deep drumming is heard from the street; folks turn their heads backwards. *The Kushites Returned* leap, sweep down the aisles, silk cloth flies in the air gleaming with silver threads, the painted dancers burst through the darkness. Spotlights follow the sounds of the bells on their wrists and ankles; they scream and sigh, and all is joy, mighty and profound, until Ariel is carried onstage on three male dancers' backs. He is clad in opulent golden cloth and his head is five feet high with billowing feathers. He jumps to the floor, undulates, and brings the Haitian spirit Damballah to the San Francisco underground theatre. The dancers had been in the aisles doing modern black American contractions and slides and swivels and things, and now they were all ancient and African and wholly non-West Coast California. It's so magic folks feel their own ancestors coming up out of the earth to be in the realms of their descendants; they feel the blood of their mothers still flowing in them, survivors of the diaspora. Ariel moves across the stage, all on the ground. Not one part of his body more than three inches off the floor—and twitching, and carrying on. The dancers all move toward him to bring his reception of Damballah to an apex—and all of a sudden, the music takes a switch, and two women looking like hootchy-coo carnie girls, 1925, begin doing an incredible belly dance behind Ariel. As they make a slow diagonal toward him from stage left, three others clad in the razzmatazz minstrel outfits of the old southern T.O.B.A. circuit start doing a soft-shoe, and the music goes crazy, and all the movements grow larger and more compelling. And all of Africa in all times is thundering through the dancers, the air. The audience doesn't exist; everybody is moving, all is not lost. Cypress laughed as she samba'd to the exit . . . niggahs still got rhythm. . . . uh-huh.

Leroy McCullough stationed himself in the corridor of Cypress' building, drawing folks coming down the street into her whoopla shindig. And drummers went up and down the stairs for a while, until everybody who was supposed to come was there, and smoking. Cypress and Sassafrass coordinated the cooking, and Malik and Guy divvied up glasses of wine: sweet, dry, red, white, tequila; and Leroy held out for keeping the beat to some funky rhythm and blues, to help dancers get into writers, and musicians get into each other, and painters to talk to someone standing next to them, and to clear the air. Because this was going to be a long affair. Women dressed in jewelry pranced around, or posed in doorways waiting to be seen or to see somebody interesting, and children played house in the middle of the foyer, saying, "Daddy is goin' on a gig tonite , , . lil one you go to sleep and when ya wake up he'll be back." Cypress gorged herself on the fullness, the life in her house, and she kept Sassafrass and Lallah busy making salads and celery with cream cheese. New chants to old river and field spirits rose up out of the gyrating crowd in the center of the house; so much clapping and stomping of feet in an Arkansas-Texas emancipation day excitement, and through the open door came the San Juan-Ponce contingent, congas strapped around their backs and clavés and tamborines in hands. Los Jibaritos brought an irresistible guaguanco into the Deep South, and some kind of New York City music evolved out of the funk and salsa. Everybody was dancing and sharing—no partners, just getting moooveddd. Sassafrass wanted to know everyone, but everyone was dancing so hard, until Ariel arrived in a white satin robe and a silver and lapis headpiece. Then something holy and quiet started happening, and folks began talking to each other . . . and Sassafrass wandered in Cypress' world.

My two big girls, Sassafrass and Cypress,

Well, looks like you are having a veritable family reunion. I wish I could be there, not just to see you both (which I really would like), but so I could finally be at one of Cypress' parties! Cypress, you be sure to introduce Sassafrass to some nice young men. She doesn't get out like she should. And Sassafrass, watch that your sister doesn't spend up all her money entertaining folks.

Isn't it wonderful, the two of you together. Cypress doing so well in that dance company and you, Sassafrass, out on your own for a while. I feel relaxed about you for a change. I don't even get shortness of breath like I used to, thinking about the earthquakes and the drugs out there in California where my two lil babies are all by themselves. Now is a good time for you both to set your minds on a good marriage.

It's not as hard as you think. Why, you just make up your mind that you are going to find a husband and one'll come along. I know this from my own experience. I set my mind on that I would be married within a year, and sure enough I was. There's nothing so heartening as a good provider and companion. And you girls realize, by now, how hard an artist's life is. So let some nice man help you.

Then all you have to worry about is your art. See, I'm not forgetting that you're both carrying on careers of your own, not at all. So when you have this party, be nice, and gracious. Let them know you're interested in family life, children, keeping house, and good company. Surely, Cypress, you wouldn't have all these parties, if you could find yourself a steady beau.

Well, all I have to do this week is a church supper and a Thursday night bridge game. You two have a good time. Mind what I told you. And dress up pretty.

*Love,
Mama*

*T*he ladies and men who might have wanted Sassafrass were too cool to seek her out so early in the evening, so Sassafrass only felt the steam heat of their glances and ended up on a cushion with Leroy McCullough, who was not at all concerned about being cool. He was a serious young man, and not given to whims of a romantic nature. He didn't even have the fear of involvement that kept most of his friends looking for a new lady; Leroy was in a woman or he wasn't, and he didn't care how much time passed between one and the next—just how much caring went down, all the time. And so he sat with Sassafrass, finding out secrets, and sharing his. Sassafrass liked the way his mouth evinced hints of sadness, how his arms were rippled with tiny criss-crossing veins, and fingers a vain woman would love to have. He was small and light-limbed, and auburn brown; all of which tripped Sassafrass out, because she was used to Mitch's towering darkness and his perennial teasing. But Leroy was actually fragile, and knowing his own delicateness, he didn't trample on Sassafrass; he kind of threw feathers and caresses in front of her every motion, so she wouldn't be hurt, and wouldn't want to tear at him, either. Sassafrass kept looking around, not used to being with another man. Leroy sensed a soprano horn around Sassafrass, and felt like whoever was playing, was playing for all he was worth. He wanted Sassafrass un-done from this other man's music, so he went off and came back with his bassoon, and tried to pull Sassafrass out of the alien melody. Sassafrass pushed herself against the wall to keep from exhibiting the pains of withdrawing from Mitch, so she could see about this new man. She fought to get Mitch out of her, but Mitch held on, and sent lyric after lyric through her marrow. Leroy laid down his horn and pulled Sassafrass up to him; held her like she might become a vapor. Then, he said, "Let's try it, huh, Sassafrass. Let's make a song, and see what we can be." Sassafrass kept holding her breath, looking through the back of her head for Mitch. Where was he? Didn't he want her at all? But she answered Leroy affirmatively, and the two of them sped up to the roof, cushions on their backs and wine in Sassafrass' bag. This was going to be a fine night, and the breeze was strong, but not chilled. So Sassafrass untied her halter and sat bare-breasted with Leroy singing to her, and pulling her breasts to the skyline.

Cypress had skedaddled with Malik to the back of the walk-in closet, so he could make a deal for some coke. Malik would do anything for Cypress except hurt her, but he was being very stubborn about having to have some blow. Finally, Cypress admitted she couldn't spare much, because she was saving the best and the larger rocks for her sister to have some money when she got back to L.A. Malik loosened up a bit; agreed to buy a miniscule portion of an ounce, which Cypress did not discount heavily, even though Malik was urging her to let him be her "good-night-kiss." Cypress laughed and joked that all they did was run together, but Malik was

Sassafrass

not smiling. He was hoping that just once Cypress would let him love her the way she ought to be, not how she prescribed. Malik wanted Cypress to know him; how she was cherished, and not obliged. And Cypress saw herself having a chance to let go of all her cynicism, and stay in business. She agreed with Malik; maybe this time she wouldn't have to keep a houseful of men busy trying to cop, and unable to deal with her except as the coke connection. Maybe this time, with a man she knew and worked with, and respected and loved in a way, she could let herself love. She knew she could. Cypress left the closet, and picked up a large antique geisha doll that sat on her dresser. She returned to Malik, and pulled off the doll's head. In the bosom were bunches of tiny aluminum rectangles Cypress liked to think of as her dowry. She gave Malik one, and shoved the headless doll in a shoebox. She and Malik sank low in the closet, ferreting out likes and dislikes, until Lallah knocked discriminately.

"Cypress, it's a long distance person-to-person call from Los Angeles."

Wiggling up, Cypress shouted, "I'm comin'."

By dawn, Cypress' house was a mass of huddled couples and threesomes under afghans and fur coats. She left Malik in a warm spot, knotted up in shawls she had made as a child. Shaking her head, Cypress pushed some weariness out of her way. "Got to make these folks some breakfast in a while; got to talk to Sassafrass." She really had to control herself to keep from shouting, "Look who's over here with . . . !", but she was actually looking for Sassafrass to tell her Mitch said she had to come home, it was time to talk. Cypress was glad and worried at the same time, because Sassafrass was her sister and should have the man she wanted, but she couldn't help thinking that Leroy was a better choice. She could just not say anything, and let Sassafrass try a new thing with Leroy; forget about that heap of blues in L.A. But she kept looking for Sassafrass, and found her sculpted into Leroy under a red and white patchwork quilt. Cypress stood over them thinking about what to do, and finally she whispered into Sassafrass' ear: "I got to talk to ya." Sassafrass woke slowly, and reluctantly followed Cypress into the kitchen. Cypress fixed some coffee and cornbread, suggesting she might have something incredible on her mind. Sassafrass was irked at this early kaffeeklatsch, and fiercely whispered, "Cypress, what do you want?" Cypress stood absolutely erect—her dancer's pose—and announced, "Mitch says you're to get on home."

Sassafrass' stomach moved into her lungs, like when someone gooses you unexpectedly. She was all caught up, and feeling the nausea of overwhelming excitement. When she could speak, she asked Cypress what else Mitch said. Cypress stood over Sassafrass, grasping her shoulders.

"Sassafrass, he didn't say anything else, just you are supposed to go on to L.A. and I am 'sposed to keep . . . now how did he say that . . . yeah. I am supposed to keep my whorish ideas to myself and send you right out of here, like you were Miss Muffet, and forget about his low-down niggah ways and you bein' in them."

Sassafrass could hardly deal with the significance of Mitch's call and Cypress' anger simultaneously, so she thought about Leroy. What would she say to him? Sassafrass rubbed her thighs, where Leroy's weight had been. Cypress kept muttering, "If you go back there, you're a real fool." Sassafrass felt herself beginning to grin . . . the touch of Leroy's lips, Mitch's wanting to be with her; the two men blending, offering Sassafrass more than

121/

she had imagined men even knew about. Tipping her head to the side and watching Cypress' every expression, Sassafrass again asked what else Mitch said exactly. Cypress started breathing real heavy, and acting like she was in a melodrama, circa 1902.

"Tell Sassafrass I love her . . . I can't exist without her . . . my life has no meaning; I am drowning in loneliness. Please tell Sassafrass I need her."

Sassafrass was amazed. "You mean he said all that?"

Cypress was livid. "You stupid ninny, Mitch didn't say nothing but 'tell Sassafrass to get her ass home.' Then he hung up the phone; I didn't even get a chance to curse his black ass."

Sassafrass bit her lip and made attempts to ignore Mitch's abrupt and cursory request for her presence. She got up to go somewhere else to think and discover some way to get that feeling back, when Leroy and Mitch were one person and no wants existed in her world. Sassafrass approached Leroy, still gentle in his slumber. She heard the music, same as the windy thrusts of their encounter on the roof: one horn beckoning, soothing, and the sounds became very old, familiar and easing like dudes on a corner hankering for a strange and rolling woman. The music echoed hot and dusky; almost blues, but cradled in possible sunlight. Sassafrass was weaving one thin willow by the sea over Leroy, and she felt herself go home. She left with the music; kissing Leroy's fingers, humming Mitch's tune.

Sassafrass jumped out of the back of the rose-printed pickup right in front of her house. Some mystical hippies had given her a ride from outside Salinas, when the bus got a flat tire. And as she made her way, awkward and giggling, toward the door, she blurted, "Well now. Somebody's swept the porch and weeded the shrubs, the

windows are washed. Mitch! Mitch . . . who you got livin'
here?" Sassafrass was a heap of tears and moans, thinking Mitch called her all the way back to L.A. just to hurt
her feelings and show her any old woman could do what
she'd been doing, and oh, shit . . . why didn't she listen
to Cypress? Mitch came through the front door, horn in
hand, and stood loosely by the rope of flowering Judas.
Sassafrass had always loved him to stand right there; the
plants whirled up the side of the house, just like her
mother's twined all through the back kitchen in Charleston. Mitch was just smiling and happy.

"Sassafrass, you came all this way here to stand outside in fronta all these Latinos and put all our nonbusi-
ness right here in the street? 'Fore you was always cryin'
'cause I didn't help you do nothin'; now you bawlin'
'cause I done it already. Will ya get your trip aligned?
Babee, listen . . ."

And Mitch drew the alto to his mouth, and Sassafrass
was grabbed up in the song, the bewitched and tortuous
mermaid song that Mitch offered her, to love her. The
alto echoed itself and notes swooned on the richness of
Mitch's breath; the air became thick as oceans by Atlan-
tis; and Sassafrass felt ten thousand hands lift her off the
earth into leap and run and breathe. Even God came
down to L.A., because the sound was pure, and Mitch
and Sassafrass were sanctified. And Albert the Great
Dane came from around back howling like he was Albert
Ayler, and the cats lay up beneath the porch.

Mitch switched into a circus parade rah-rah, and the
whole family jigged around the house two or three times,
for Sassafrass. She pulled all her belongings just
through the front door, shooed the dog away, and vi-
brantly led Mitch to the long-unshared two-poster bed
that almost shimmered this particular day, because the
afternoon sun was picking his way through the laced and

diaphanous curtains, same as the tiny buds of flowering
Judas were coming through the hole behind the rocking
chair. And Sassafrass and Mitch discovered the joy in
themselves—again—and Mitch jerked up once because
Sassafrass was laughing like a spook-house demon; she
got enough words out to sing, a la Robeson, "My lawd
what a mornin' . . . oh lawd, what a mo-ooorrr-nnnn
. . ." and they consecrated spirits until crickets began
messing with the sunset.

Everything was just hustle and bustle. Sassafrass was
busy putting her things in old and new places, Mitch was
packing his instruments for a gig later on, and Cleo, the
neighbor (former Merchant Marine), was yapping away
about travelling the world. And folks kept calling because Sassafrass was back. She, who thought she would
never be missed, was bowled over by such reception.
Even Howard and Otis came by and managed to be
pleasant. And Sassafrass forgot she ever had left. Mitch
was so healthy and interested in assisting her, she just
couldn't get over it; any of it. She went up to Mitch and
pulled his shirt, stage-whispering.
  "So this is what happens when you get to play your
horn for money, huh? You get generous and committed
to livin'—is that right?"
  Mitch laughed inside his throat and lifted Sassafrass
'til her head touched the ceiling (which was low), and
Valentinoed back, "Mamselle, the paid *artiste* has no
worries. Mamselle, you are bein' supported—and I say
this with modesty—you are bein' upheld by the only
horn player in the only combo in the only club in Comp-
ton, California that hires non-Texas blues bands. Now
that's not the Village Vanguard or the East, or the Afro-
American Livin' Theatre, but we got soul . . . an' we get
paid. Below union scale, but we get paid. An' we can't

play free, but we can play funky. We on a double bill with some old dudes could show ninety-eleven young horn players what dudes are, just by standin' up all beat an' crooked. And I tell ya, Sassafrass, we gonna get it on tonight—for you. I'ma do every blues lick I ever knew, and I don't want you to arrange nothin', don't want ya to carry nothin', I just want ya to groove on the rhythm. Same as all that ol'-fashioned knottin' and tyin' you be doin', only it's me. Sassafrass, I know why you so ol' fashioned and respectful of the old folks—'cause they know where we come from, and how to make do. And can't a soul down at the place tell a holler from a scream, but we do be gettin' holy."

By this time Sassafrass was beaming, and squirming because she was still in the air. Mitch let her down right where he could pinch her ass, and it wasn't until they were in the car that she got a chance to tell him about the cocaine Cypress gave her to sell so she could invest the money in the artists' community in Louisiana, and they could get on to a new way of living.

Mitch never got excited about having to get rid of two ounces of coke quick-like, but he didn't ever say it wasn't all right, either, because you do what you got to, and $15.00 maximum per nite wasn't going to send anybody anywhere close to New Orleans for at least a year. And Sassafrass was right about L.A.: it wasn't a place for free Africans to be being free in, especially with Mitch's record, and the way he towered over every living thing in sight except for the buildings out by Century Boulevard, and of course, the L.A. County Jail. But something was not clicking, and Mitch decided to wait and see. As always, the Arkansas Spot was hopping as much as it could, with some gut-bucket jukebox spirit just crying how his woman done left him high and dry. Mitch met the rest of his band at the end of the bar, and

Ntozake Shange

Sassafrass sat in an old splintered chair, like the kind in Polish lunchrooms down by the warehouses. She was right at ease; red-checkered napkins were tucked under the ice container in the back of the place, and she was sitting nattily in a claret satin and velvet dress Mitch had traded a painting for. Sassafrass scavenged the bar looking for another past in the faces of the workers carrying on for Friday's sake, and the regulars nobody could mess with. She felt the rancor of Cypress' vendetta against the blues, and her own affinity for slow low-down tearin-ya-up singing, and guitars pulling through hairs on her stomach to hold onto her insides so she could swear she knew the pain, the truth of her existence. As ladies in skinny-heeled tipping shoes straddled in with a housewife's "I'm-out-for-the-night" switch, and young working girls in all the latest, cheapest clothes, padded in makeup and bangles, sat swivel legged in chairs facing the bar where men—younger than the law allowed —tossed scant shots of whiskey down throats scratching in newly pressed collars, and old dudes with grease relentless under the nails and those heavy working-walking-carrying shoes leaned over each other, Sassafrass began a conversation with Mamie Smith . . .

. . . who had just come out of the bathroom, and was busy straightening the plumes of lime and lavender that grazed her heavily waxed coiffure. Her silken dress clung to her broad hips and full bosom like she was a hefty Cotton Club dancer . . . on her arms were aeons of pre-depression plastic bracelets, and she smelled of day-opened scotch and fresh perfume.

As she let her ass reach for the chair nearest Sassafrass, she laughed one of those raspy drunk laughs, and patted Sassafrass' shoulder, saying, "Chile, if this wasn't one of your visions I'd be wearin' the same second-hand white lady's dress as you . . . and I wouldn't hardly be havin' no just-done hair, or these plenty bracelets

*. . . why I probably would be lookin' to one of these men
to keep me company."*

Sassafrass moved to hold Mamie's hand, and the
woman jumped like she got the spirit, and strutted in
place.

*"I'll eat pork if I want to; I'll paint both my lips red.
I ain't goin' to heaven when I'm dead. And Garvey can't
save me 'cause I ain't ready to go home . . . no I don't
want no sympathy from any of y'all. I gotta sing this
low; I gotta share this burden; I gotta pay the Devil his
due. Get outta my way! Can't ya see? I'm sufferin'; I'm
bringin' ya tears your mama shed, that terrible loneliness in the middle of her bed. Her hands worn all tough,
and her body what-all misery could lay on it . . . get
outta my way. Gotta sing this sorrow's tale, and I'm
alright, and mad. And I'm alright, and sorry, how the
river floods. Lawd, I'm bringin' ya the fears of your kin
in this ravaged land, and I gotta sing this low. I'm
forsaken—ya know it—don't bring me no kind words,
bring me a full shot o' gin, and let me roll a lil truth
on ya. Honey, just look at yourself, all innocent and soft
. . . I'm a hard mama and can't nobody take it from me,
less'n I want to give it up. I bet ya work a lot with your
hands and make pretty things and don't have no chirren,
either . . . well, I had me a bunch o' chirren and as many
men, and I still went on singin' in taverns or the street
. . . honey, I didn't care, not like folks expect a mama
to care. I gotta whole world fulla chirren, and tell 'em
what's a blues about . . . then I let 'em be. Yeah then
I let 'em be."*

Mamie sat down again, and effused that heavy scent
of trouble in mind. Sassafrass huddled over her, fixing
the tousled feathers and patting Mamie's wide cheeks,
until the Southern songstress dissolved amid the clatter
and excitement of Mitch's group, setting up . . .
"Ladies and Gentlemen." The owner of the bar was

speaking as proper as he knew how. "This night we gonna present a local group, with some Arkansas blood —hahaha—called Stick-Up, and ya favorite down-home duo, Washboard Sam and Ironin' Board Slim, so y'all be sure an' stick around 'cause we are gonna be hoppin'. Alright, alright . . . y'all take it."

And Stick-Up, led by Mitch, was corralled by the same folks that had been sitting and styling and eyeing each other. Now everybody was ready to swing, and Mitch broke out in some King Curtis solo. Then came the traps, then the electric bass—sort of loud—then the trumpet, just teasing, and the whole sound was like a James Brown Revue in Fauquier County, Virginia. Thick pushing, wailing, and Sassafrass could catch Mitch's incessant experiments.

He wasn't doing it exactly like we all know it, but exactly like it could be, and still smoking. Folks were doing all kinds of dancing, rubbing up and down, showing off, being cool, every old thing was going down. Exactly thirty minutes later, Mitch signalled for a whanging end to the set, and the folks were disturbed; they wanted to keep on dancing and forgetting and dancing. But the management only allowed thirty-minute sets, because on Fridays and Saturdays clients had to buy at least two drinks a set, so Mitch's group climbed down from the podium (which really reminded Sassafrass of pictures of old slave auction stands, but the thought was so odd she threw it out). Sassafrass sauntered up to Mitch to give the music back to him, round the back of his left ear. Mitch smiled and was actually very proud of himself, but he insisted Sassafrass catch the next act, because it was important.

Up on the podium, two worn-out not-in-a-hurry old men were getting their act together; the heavyset one standing over the ironing board, the thinner, smaller one sitting on a chair with a washboard in his hands. They were smiling and joking back and forth. Sassafrass looked at Mitch inquisitively. "What they gonna do?" Mitch beamed, and motioned for her to keep watching. Then Slim, at the ironing board, stomped his foot hard on the stage: 1 . . . 2 . . . 3 . . . 4, and all this music started coming out of the place. With the washboard came the melody, and little riffs and songs like a good woman sings at night. On the ironing board was a mean rhythm section—yes, a rhythm section—and the two old-timers tore the place down. Folks were just hopping, jumping up and down, or making elaborate personal statements about themselves with their bodies. Sashaying or beckoning—daring somebody to come and get it. And Sassafrass was ecstatic; she didn't know what to do with herself. She was just dancing and falling back to the South, to the shanties and sweet cornbread, and she wanted to kiss the feet and fingers of Washboard Sam and Ironin' Board Slim, because they were music . . . they were the truth.

Suddenly Mitch tugged Sassafrass' sleeve. "Come here, Sassafrass. I gotta talk to ya. Some dudes just came in lookin' for me. I owe 'em some money from when I was usin' an' I gotta get outta here, or pay up. Could I exchange that coke? I swear to ya we'll still get to Louisiana this year . . . Sassafrass please . . . I don't wanna haveta deal with these suckers anymore."

Sassafrass was stiff and bewildered for a minute. She had lost the evilness of their reality; she hadn't been part of anything but joy, and here was something else. She kept thinking she was lost in the depths of Hell and nothing would get her out of L.A. Then she looked up almost smiling and surprised herself. She didn't care about her dreams, if her truth—her real life—was hurting, and Mitch was real life, and needing from her something she could give, and did.

"Sure. Get rid of it. It's bad karma anyway. How we

gonna go to a new life commune on ol' dead life money?"

And the two of them got back to their business of being conjured by the rooted blues. Every once in a while, Washboard Sam would scream:

"Goddamn chile. Come on. Goddamn babeee, come on. Come on. Heah. Ohhhhhh, goddammmmm chile, come heah. I got it, heah."

My dearest Sassafrass,

I was so glad to hear that you are staying in Los Angeles for a while longer. It's not that I don't want you nearer to me, only I don't think it's a good idea to take the white folks to court to get back land they've owned since before the war, to give to Negroes who are descendants of slaves.

I think I understand what you are trying to do, but remember we all have to live in this country together, and I believe that the Negro people have enough land to get by with right now. As a matter of fact, did you know that one Geechee after another is selling little parcels of land right off those islands? The white folks are going to build resorts and hotels like in Puerto Rico; won't that be something?

Anyway, that should show you that Negroes don't want any more land, they are selling the land they do have! Why don't you all get some land from the Colored that are selling? That way you could leave these white folks alone. It seems downright unpatriotic of you, Sassafrass, to attack the white folks in the middle of one of their wars. If you must come back to the South, why don't you stay here?

Charleston is as lovely as ever, and you could go out to eat, or sit anywhere you want, any place, any time. It's not like when you were a little girl, not at all.

Maybe this holiday, Kwanza, is not as bad as I thought. When you said you weren't having Christmas, I kept wondering where I had failed. Still, as long as it's a religious ceremony with feasts and gifts like Christmas, I guess it'll be okay. Why does it go on for so many days? You haven't explained all of it to me yet . . . I was attempting to tell the Bowdry sisters about your goings on, but I just don't have enough information. Is the Maulana the same as the Savior, or is he like a minister, for you all, I mean?

Here is a recipe I want you to have, so there won't be too much heathen in your Christmas this year (I found a wonderful way to make a dressing for turkey with hot sausage, cornbread, and peanut butter that's supposed to be African but I know you don't eat pork).

Mama's Kwanza Recipe (for Sassafrass): Duck with Mixed Oyster Stuffing

1 duck, 5–7 pounds, cleaned & seasoned
1 pan cornbread
2 tablespoons butter
½ cup celery, chopped
Salt & fine black pepper to taste
1 medium onion, chopped
1 teaspoon paprika
1 ground red pepper pod
1 dozen oysters (medium)
1 cup pecans, chopped

Wet the cornbread, break into bits and fry in the butter with the celery and onion. Add seasonings. As mixture gets crisp, add oysters & pecans. Stuff your duck & bake in a 450° oven for 15 minutes, then lower to 350° and bake 15 minutes for each pound. Baste every 15 minutes. Don't forget to cover the bottom of the pan with water, and be sure to keep the duck tightly covered until the last 15 minutes, when the skin can brown.

Now, that seems like a dish packed full of love and history to me. Send me the other patterns you've been working on. I was trying to see if I could set up my warps like yours to make "art" things for Christmas sales to Mrs. Fitzhugh's friends. Charleston doesn't have the sophistication of California, but things change, even your mama (smile).

Love you so much, my oldest daughter,

Mama

P.S. Are you sure that Mitch has talent? I looked at those drawings over and over . . . can't say I know what they are about. You be sure he loves you as much as you love him. It's better for a man to love you a little more than you love him . . . take my word.

133/

dancin is the movement of oceans/
the caress of many lovers in canyons
laced wit poppies n coca leaves/
dancin is union of spirits layed
to rest among splinterin shells
n fires of adoration in the heat
of comets n volcanoes/ dancin
is how i love/ how i share carin
how did mama say it

"Cypress, didn't I tell you to come straight home from school to help me with this cloth? You've been standing round that ballet class, haven't you? Ballet is for white girls; now, can't you understand? Your ass is too big and your legs are too short, and you can't afford all those shoes and special clothes . . . but if you must be just like my sister and hanker after classical movements and grace, I'll send you up to New York. Effie is working with some Negro woman doing ballet; I took care of her long enough for her to take you for a while . . . I'll write her; see if all that white folks' mess doesn't fix your hard-headed behind for a minute . . . Cypress, I don't want to see any of my

*children hanging round any crackers down heah to learn
anything. If you want to study dance, you've got to wait
'til I can send you to Effie. If you don't, I'ma fix you so
you won't be able to move anything at all, not a muscle!
Now get started on that tapestry for Mrs. Fitzhugh, it's got
to be done by Spring, before you leave for New York. And
I'll be damned if you don't come back some kind of ballerina . . . all proper. "*

Then they worked, and Cypress made a secret promise to her mother: to dance as good as white folks and
to find out the truth about colored people's movements,
because she knew dancing was in her blood . . . every
step.

Effie wore a lot of makeup and lived six flights up on
the East Side in New York City near Brooklyn, sort of.
Cypress didn't go to school, she went to class and rehearsal with Effie, and she sweat and arched and cried
because she hurt. She tried to learn French, and the
difference between modern and classical ballet.

Effie was impatient and mean about dancing, because
it's got to be right, and Cypress went on. Her body was
tight, her mind astounded by dancing in New York, no
fresh food, funny languages, old Ukrainian women looking in garbage cans, the moon hidden by concrete offices,
Effie entertaining dancers and singers 'til the next rehearsal . . . and always more to learn, more energy to
find; and no congratulations about getting better. She
was almost sixteen, and didn't know anybody under
twenty-five.

Cypress gave her life to dancing, reducing complex
actions to the curve of her wrist. Ariel Moröe took her
into his troupe, The Kushites Returned, and immersed
her in the ways of pre-Egyptian Nile culture, and Cy-

press was discovering the movements of the colored people that had been lost. Year after year Ariel's company almost starved, but they danced nine hours a day, and moved all over the country playing audiences rallied behind the sit-in movements and Equal Opportunity for Colored Folks. The Kushites Returned played itsy-bitsy "lil ol Southern towns," and introduced factory workers, sharecroppers, doctors, and church-women to the brazen mystical motions of black Nile dance.

Cypress took up with some of the musicians in the troupe, and she would listen and soar toward indefinite heavens when they played. Her dance took on the essence of the struggle of colored Americans to survive their enslavement. She grew scornful of her years of clamoring for ballet, and grew deep into her difference. Her ass and her legs she used like a colored girl; when she danced, she was alive; when she danced, she was free.

The Kushites Returned were just outside Chicago. In fifteen more hours they were going to hit New York City for the first time in three years. Cypress had started painting her nails aqua and mauve, while the five-car caravan of dancers waited for tire checks and gasoline. She wasn't really there, on the road; she was still in her house in San Francisco, and everyone in the company sensed her reluctance to join them in eager anticipation of the Only City—New York. She had said no more than thirty sentences in the four days they had been on the road. Ariel Moröe had had her switched from car to car, thinking she needed more variety on the road than anyone else, but it hadn't worked.

Cypress wasn't with them. This decision she'd made, to stop dealing and dance for a living, was more frightening than she had any reason to believe it would be. For

months she'd looked forward to the day when she could
say, "No, I don't have a thing," and mean it. She rubbed
her bosoms like she knew her grandma would have on
such a hot day. Patting her chest, to remind herself that
she had saved enough to stay out of business for a few
months; she did have a chance to make it as a dancer;
she did not have to worry. She carried traveller's checks.
No more dealing. That was a relief, for a while. When
she sat still, she thought of her kitchen, and Lallah and
Dulce and Maureen, the women she'd danced with
. . . her friends, whom Ariel had decided not to take on
tour.

Cypress was the only woman with Ariel's troupe doing
the swing tour through Washington, Philly, and New
York. Ariel had said he could pick up some more girls
on a swing basis wherever they worked, but he needed
the men. "Humph," Cypress kept shaking her head.
"There's four dudes wit us couldn't do a run-run-leap
without fallin' on themselves." But they were men. And
men were prized in dance.

And men riding in cars for days and days talk a lot,
about being prized and sought after, being badder than
thunder in the mountains; and Cypress listened and
listened. What could she say? Men talking to men
about being men who like men and occasionally take a
woman. Cypress tweezed her eyebrows, pushed cuti-
cles, braided her hair, slept, stared out the windows,
kept quiet, and remembered too many men. Long men
standing by trees in parks. Smart men being glib. Men
taking off her clothes. Men flirting with each other
when they danced with her. Men eating her food; men
in her bed. Men holding her, leaving her wet and
lonely. Cypress didn't say much cross-country. She
remembered and nestled in the back seat. With her
journal, she talked to herself.

Ntozake Shange

JOURNAL ENTRY #48

everybody i know has lost they mind
sometimes i wish i was crazy too/ then i cd get some
sleep/ this way i keep lookin round
waiting for X to jump
tryin to catch Y for he picks up the one-nite-stand/
for a second time/ imaginin Z cuttin his wrists
ABC & D runnin naked on 42nd street . . .
everybody i know is recoverin from a bad affair
wishin for mister right
lookin for miz true
& i cant get any rest
i'm so tired & nerve worn
when the antelopes & gazelles peeped thru my
window
i invited them in/ the conversations i was havin
weren't important enuf to exclude animals of note/
i bit my tongue for mentionin jean harlow to freddie
washington
my friends are ridiculous/ i haveta change my
associations/
talk abt fantasy runnin wild/ please dont anybody
say/
"& this is yr life."

At 5th Street and Second Avenue the company set up
house in a three-room draft. When Malik was turned out,
then Bruce, then Pedrito, Cypress moved her things into
the closet and stayed there at night after rehearsal. The
lovemaking was so active and one-dimensional she preferred pulling coats round her ears, and sleeping with
her face to the corner. But it was too much, when Ariel
screamed across the studio to the new women:
   "You whores go off with Cypress 'til ya know what in

the hell you're doin'. I don't need no clumsy pussy out in public."

Cypress had enough, and moved in with two women she'd met at some dance classes in the West Village.

Celine and Ixchell belonged to a women's dance collective called Azure Bosom that worked out of Ovary Studio in the Bowery. Celine adored Cypress and had hit on her to move in the first time they showered together after point class. Celine was thin like a puma, with mahogany-tinted, pure flesh. No eyebrows or hair on her head; just rich skin and line. Celine usually painted her cheeks and eyes with bright geometric shapes. Her lips were always deep purple. Ixchell liked crêpe and velvet dresses to sit right on her Panamanian ass, where her two braids bounced when she walked. Ixchell had taken off her eyebrows too; there were tufts of ostrich and macaw feathers above her eyes, and earrings that attached to the ring in her nose, so she was a gliding and jeweled thing. Ixchell and Celine smiled a lot and never covered their bodies with arms, or slumped carelessly into a seat or neglected to breathe evenly and deeply when anyone was looking at their bodies, but they never saw men on a personal basis.

Actually, someone had said not one of the women in Azure Bosom saw men, at all, anywhere. Celine and Ixchell took Cypress in and gave her the window-room looking at the Brooklyn Bridge. Cypress was beside herself, in a woman's house at last. Everywhere—in the bathroom, the hallway and living room, all along the studio walls—were photographs, paintings, drawings, and sculptures of women by women. All third-world women. Cypress saw herself everywhere she looked. Nothing different from her in essence; no thing not woman. And she loved it.

Celine cooked for friends the same as Cypress had in San Francisco, but now for breakfast and evening wine came women. Writers, dancers, printers, painters, and filmmakers, beautiful like a woman appreciates. Courteous, good-smelling and clean, and each one unique. Cypress met more women in three days with Celine and Ixchell than she had ever known. And they talked about art and New York and food. About God and Venus intercepting Uranus and men. Cypress never knew that women as lovely as these appeared to be and as complete as these appeared to be could have so much to say about men. Cypress had nothing to say about them. She wanted to talk to women who were about being women; she didn't want to talk about men. Not here in her woman-being space. And how they talked so perfectly, in tact, inscrutably desirable and bitter:

"Well, if ya could'a seen that dude's face when I kissed Elva on the corner by the theatre. He looked like I had cut off his dick. So I pulled open her blouse a lil an' licked her titty. God. He looked like he was gonna puke." (titter, titter)

"Yeah, but what good would a man do somebody like me? I write my own things and pay my rent. 'Cause somebody's got a penis mean I gotta want it?"

"I develop all my own film and mat my own stuff. Can you imagine those fellas in the Puerto Rican collective askin' me do I wanna help them set up their show in the Super Señor Gallery?"

"If he ever asks me to dance wit his faggot ass again I'll tear off alla my clothes an' sit on his head wit both legs wide open."

"I told my daughter if she wanted to be with her daddy she better go on and do it now, 'cause there ain't gonna be no more men in my life ever, is there, Berte?"

"Not in my life."

"Emotionally underdeveloped species." (hahahaha)
"I certainly can't uoc one."
"What for?"
"What could they do for us?"
"I could do that for ya, mama!" (laughter)
"It's sad, isn't it. One-half the world is them."
Cypress loved looking at them. So soft and delicate. She didn't listen long; she didn't want to speak of men in her woman-space. She looked as if she were in a silent film, and watched Azure Bosom dance a female dance. A gender dance. A dance of ovaries and cervix uncovered and swelling, menses falling like waterfalls in a golden forest. A dance of women discovering themselves in the universe. She. Her. Hers. Us. Cypress didn't listen too much. She felt connected to these women among women as she had never felt around any man. She loved them in a primal way; being able to touch and fondle and kiss as if one body enclosed them all. And they danced and worked, and publicized the Azure Bosom concert: "Vulva Dreams."

There was nothing straight at Ovary Studio. Everything was round, curving, textured, and dense. No sense of the possibility of masculinity existed. The ceiling was covered with moss, like pubic hair. The aisles of the theatre arena moved like errant streams. Everywhere there was flow. Azure Bosom had quite a following in New York City. They were regarded as the thrust of the future for women in dance, articulating what women had never acknowledged: our bodies are not our destiny, but all freeing-energy. Azure Bosom brought many women to tears, to joy . . . a sense of quiet easiness they had never known. Because Azure Bosom had given so many women so much of themselves, many many women came to the opening, "Vulva Dreams" was what they were after.

Ntozake Shange

PLACES

Azure Bosom moved down the winding aisles in slow motion, making "shhh" and quiet "ahhh" sounds. They seemed to lose all skeletal form. The women were clouds billowing, unfurling smoke rings, and "shhhh" and "ahhhhhh" embraced all souls and caressed and tumbled over lips and there was a holy warmth, another communion. A sensual joining of strangers . . . the sound of women loving themselves.

As they approached the stage, Azure Bosom began a series of prolonged contractions that pushed their bodies irregularly in space, until the tension in their spines was vigorous and filled with danger. The hushing sounds became screams and the haunting "ahhhh" was a pelvic groan like trembling oceans on a still night. They rolled across the stage erratically, like women possessed, and their sounds were beings collapsing in mirrors, and someone of them sighed for "mama." Then a chorus of all the different times and voices for that one woman issued forth like the burning bush, and it went on, the cry for "mama," until Celine made a gesture for silence.

And then there was celebration. Celebration of menses; of why she can be daughter, why she can be mother. How girl from woman. And the widely esteemed Azure Bosom puberty rite began. The first lighting other than candles blazed out, red. The women began to touch their thighs, make like they were smelling their fingers, seeing something wondrous come from themselves. Their hips cut into space, became familiar with sex. And suddenly Stevie Wonder's "Here I Am, Babeee, Signed, Sealed and Delivered" blasted throughout the Ovary Studio. Accepting menstruation as the key to womanhood, what made bosoms and ass possible, why mama exists, and love among us. The women in Azure Bosom became the female body exalted. As the Stevie Wonder song faded out, the women made clicking sounds with their tongues and rubbed their thighs and crotches in a moving kick series out of the arena, leaving the audience to continue the ritual until every woman greeted her flowing blood and rounded hips with unbounded thanks.

CLITORIS
Choreographed by Ixchell Buenavilla
Music by the Marvalettes, "Forever"

From the far right of the round stage Ixchell slithered and waxed, seeming to pull all that was pain and disappointment out of her body. Her hands and feet articulated wanting something that was not there, reaching to place some constantly evasive element in some other than herself, while her torso heaved and contracted toward her heart like she was a cavern or a prisoner. She was the cave and the light. And all women forced to nourish someone other than themselves were dangling in her fingers, watching themselves dissolve in another breath. Ixchell seemed to die right on the stage. So intense and stultifying were her motions that she grabbed the whole of the theatre into her suffering, and allowed no lapses of relief from complete suppression of self. The final posture of the dance was a contracted spread-eagle: hands, feet, knees, and neck flexed. Absolute despair in the archetypal sprawl of the ravaged woman. Ixchell drew out the torture until the last light was off. Her shadow suggested a four-day-old corpse.

HOW DO SHE DO
Choreographed by Celine
Music by the Isley Brothers, "Who's That Lady?"

In slightly spangled tights and Apache-dancer skirts, Azure Bosom sashayed through the audience like She

143/

who is not only looking, but She who has found an eye
to taunt, to tease, to promise heaven in the switch of a
hip, and bosom bounce. "How Do She Do" is the coquette Erzulie, introduced to modern lovers unaccus-
tomed to pure pleasure of flesh and spirit combined.
This She is not a body in silk panties, but a body in silk
panties enjoying being in silk panties and surveyed
walking down 125th Street in silk panties with sunlight
streaming through her legs. This is She to love bright
and quick, and hold like a vapor of a lovely woman
walking through the subway train, who passed on to
another; but when she was there ... when she was there,
there was all woman ever knew to be. Azure Bosom
obviously loved this dance. And there was reason to love
the freeing of the coquette from the responsibility of
breaking men's hearts, driving them to compulsive
desires and guilt. This She was free of all that, and
allowed women to linger in their own eroticism; to be
happy with loving themselves. Celine was center front in
her own dance. She was the awesome and spry carnal
connection to the spirit of infinite giving, the flirt gives
so much pleasure to those who know how to receive
without taking, and Celine led Azure Bosom's hips, ass,
tits, neck, and mouth right into everyone's soul. She was
doing more than all right; she was doing all she could
do to make everyone enjoy her simply being beautiful
and ready.

"How Do She Do" grew into a communal "Come
Dance with Me." Azure Bosom pulled folks out of the
crowd, onto the stage to be raucous and seduce with
women moving. What they wanted in the first place: to
be, and share women moving. They worked, and "Vulva
Dreams" became real.
    Any woman who liked women at all would have loved

them after Azure Bosom's concert. "Vulva Dreams" was the sucking of a ripe plum or chilled strawberry to any possible woman who likes fresh and natural growing things. And the party at Celine's, Ixchell's, and Cypress' was a delightful buffet. For women, all kinds of women. Not just the super-chic and independent ones like Celine, who were so svelte only the dresses moving in the dark let someone know there was a body, but others rounder than Ixchell and more heavily bangled than Cypress. Women in trousers, gabardine and silk. Women with moustaches and Camels, more subtle types with Shermans and boots. Women with big stomachs and big tits. Women looking like Smokey Robinson and women looking like Miriam Makeba. Somebody being fiery like La Lupe. And some women who didn't even know this was an Azure Bosom party, and women couldn't come as women but only as women and: women and jewelry and attitude and talent and ennui and good taste and body. Azure Bosom was one thing, Azure Bosom's parties were something else; more like a slave market where everybody was selling herself.

Cypress fit right in. Since she had been in New York City she'd been dancing much harder than in San Francisco; she didn't have such a peasant figure any more, nor the casual attire she'd craved on the West Coast. She was actually looking very expensive and terribly unapproachable, which was the look for this particular crowd. But Cypress didn't really know why she should put herself up for auction to be run off with by some woman she didn't know, any more than she understood what cruelty had to do with a good time. And since she wasn't having one, she left to take a walk. She was waving goodbye to something Brooklyn and Caribbean in a scarlet satin skirt and golden flowers pasted to her fleeting tits, as something Manhattan and subdued-colored snarled, "I don't know who it's gonna be tonite, but I'ma fix her so she won't never want nothin' but what I got . . ."

Cypress was so upset she walked all the way to 72nd Street before she realized someone was walking with her. A woman in bluejeans and gold hoops all the way round her ears was mostly what Cypress saw. They didn't say anything; they just kept walking, and when they looked at each other, the tension of being strangers lessened. Cypress turned to walk east on 96th, so did the woman. Finally Cypress took a deep breath.

"Okay. Mama, what's up?"

"Well. I saw you leave Ixchell's before I could talk to ya, an' I wanted to talk to ya, an' ya looked like ya needed someone to talk to an' thought there was no one there. So I followed ya."

"What did you want to talk about. I'm not lookin' for a quick an' easy, alright?"

"Hey. Hey. I just wanted to know ya; I don't wanna do anythin' to ya. I can't stand those vampire bitches either, but I was lonely so I thought I'd try to make some new friends, while my lady is in Europe."

They were still walking, and now at First Avenue and 86th Street, Cypress and this woman, Idrina, went to have a glass of wine.

Idrina was a dancer, too. She and Cypress focused most of their attention on being third-world female dancers in the United States, and being disgusted with the way a lot of Celine and Ixchell's friends conducted themselves in the world. Idrina, who was quite delicate herself, found Cypress' indignation and disillusionment about being a dancer in New York City charming. Absolutely charming. They had two or three half-decanters of wine, in two or three bars, before Idrina walked Cypress back to the Bowery. Somewhere between the mid-East

Side and Canal Street, Idrina found a slightly tousled
flower for Cypress' hair, a perfectly shaped rock for
Cypress' good luck, a stray pigeon feather for Cypress'
ear, an empty window frame for Cypress' weaving, and
a way of putting her tiny hand round the back of Cypress' neck so Cypress just smiled.

JOURNAL ENTRY #151

> *yesterday my bosoms*
> > *kept   fallin out*
> *my shirts*
> > *move easily when i turn*
> *the right nipple   wiggles*
> *but/*
> *idrina say*
> *"what's a lil titty 'mong friends?"*

Cypress and Idrina, dancing-growing-loving in New
York.
"Ya wanna dance in New York, huh. Alright, ya do
the toe-thang, don't'cha? Heah we go . . ."
In a vast and deep studio cluttered with brown women
and some men, Cypress tried to enjoy point, the lift of
ballet. And Idrina made it so easy. Whenever M'sieur
Tomas screamed in his Bronxite Southern drawl, "You
colored people better get it toooo-gethaaaah. If you
caaaan't dance, Mizzzz Thaaaang, get the hell outta my
class, honey," Cypress would cringe and miss a step.
Idrina would touch her arm and whisper, "He's got to
teach whoever comes in here. You know you're a dancer;
you can't pay him no mind. He knows more than us, and
he just trips. Not everybody has enough nerve to dance;
that shoutin' builds it in somebody who's really gonna
dance. Don't you trip 'cause he's gone out."
During stretches M'sieur Tomas tried to push Cy-

press' knee to her ear, and Cypress took as much pull as she could, until she yanked her leg down and cooed, "M'sieur, you gotta give me a few days to catch up on your technique. I know my leg will go up there if I keep comin' here."

And Idrina winked, as Cypress turned back to the barre and pliéd and pliéd, trying to make her leg her own again. From one class to the next Idrina filled Cypress in on the idiosyncrasies of all the teachers:

"Alfredo is gonna hit on ya, right away. He is the one teachin' Angolan dance. And Pierre Aubignon teachin' Congolese doesn't like inhibited Afro-American dancers. So let your hips go in there or he'll be on your case from now until. And Miz Wilson's jazz motto is: 'loose thighs, women,' so wear your sweat pants and plastic leggings if ya go to her. And don't let anyone get you down."

"But Idrina. You don't believe in all this pressure and 'professionalism,' do ya? I mean, that somebody should not be able to dance 'cause they can't remember steps quick, or 'cause they weigh ten pounds more than someone else. And all that hostility. You've seen Ariel, haven't ya? He doesn't do nothin' compared to these snotty, nose-in-the-air teachers here."

"Well. No. I love dancin', that's all. If somebody knows somethin' that's gonna make me dance more and better, I wanna know what that is. And yeah, I guess I do wanna be as close to perfect as I can be, but I want as many people to dance as want to. I want the whole world to dance, but dancers are a strange breed, Cypress —don'tchu know that. We are compulsive-obsessive, I think that's the phrase. We dance all day, move round dancers, in our spare time go see other dancers and for fun we go dancin'. There's no way to make us less intense, unless we fall in love . . . but not with another dancer."

148/

So Cypress learned to see other people as themselves, and not as threats to her person. What somebody was doing was what they were doing, but not necessarily to her. And she waited for Idrina every morning at the 14th Street station, so they could go dance together all day. Eat a light supper. And fall out in each other's arms at night.

Idrina knew some things Cypress didn't know: where to eat in the City; which piers to visit in the wee hours of the night and watch the waves and sunrise. How to love a woman like Cypress—something Cypress hadn't known; that she could be loved, because she'd never let anyone close enough. Yet Idrina seemed to move right in and slay the dragons Cypress had spouting "don't touch me," simply by looking at her. Holding her. Finding little things for her, going to hear music with her. Walking with her. Kissing her scalp, rubbing her legs, making her breakfast, taking her picture. Being there when Cypress came into the room. Idrina knew some things Cypress didn't know: loving is not always the same as having. And Idrina loved Cypress, but not to have . . . and Cypress didn't know that.

But Ixchell knew something more than Idrina had imagined. Idrina's lady was on her way back from Amsterdam. While Cypress was visiting her house, saying hello to Celine and company, and getting ready to go meet Idrina, Ixchell exclaimed,

"I just got a letter from Holland. Laura is gonna be home next week. I guess we'll be seein' more of ya then, Cypress. Make the next few days last. Idrina and Laura rarely come out, when they are both in town." There was a vicious silence; then Celine murmured,

"I'm sure Idrina told you how she hates us 'vampire girls,' didn't she? And how honest carin' is all that's important, and that humans shouldn't use or abuse one another, especially not women, huh? And did she find you a flower and play the very wooden flute on Grant's tomb . . ."

Ixchell was watching. From some part of herself she had no control over, she tried to patch the wounds.

"Oh, Celine. You know Cypress could see through that. She just wanted some attention while she was here. Cypress doesn't need anybody so much she just can't leave 'em. She never lets anyone into her."

Cypress knew better than to flinch or cry out in the presence of dangerous animals. Celine and Ixchell were gnawing on her bones as she closed the front door.

Idrina knew something was wrong, but Cypress was a moody woman and kept a lot of secrets. So Idrina left her to herself, even though they were together for hours. Idrina played Kyoto recordings and read to Cypress from the Bhagavad-Gita after class. Cypress had left again for an imagined Shangri-la where she was safe from hurt and her own feelings. She wasn't with Idrina, and Idrina knew that and didn't like it. Idrina believed in being where you are when you're there and someplace else, when you get there. So she confronted Cypress with an unfamiliar tone.

"I never promised ya anythin'. So what are ya doin'?"

"I'm being reasonably unhappy, so I won't have to be ridiculous when Laura comes back next week."

"How could I have thought our wonderful friends would let me take care of my own business?"

Cypress was standing by the window, looking at the cars, becoming steely and attempting to ignore everything Idrina was saying:

"Why are ya gonna be unhappy, Cypress? I do love you. I really love you and I'm not abandoning you to some lonesome and miserable life. I'll be in your life, I just won't be there all the time . . . but I'll be there whenever you need me as a friend, or lover. So don't draw away. Don't leave."

"Oh yeah. You're gonna be there all right, when Laura goes out of town."

"You knew she was comin' back. I always let you know that."

"Yeah. Well. She's comin' back and you can have her. But not me, I can't do it. I can't do it. Why didn't you leave me alone . . ."

Idrina moved closer to Cypress and caressed her face. "You didn't want to be left alone. I didn't want to leave you alone, and you love someone now, don't you. You didn't hold back and make fun and games. You didn't ignore your spirit and be someone you aren't 'cause you didn't have the faith to be yourself. Ahhhh, Cypress. Can't you see I've been doin' this 'us' with you. With you, not to you."

"Then that makes me one big damn jackass, doesn't it. Helpin' somebody hurt my feelings. That's so intelligent and self-sufficient, I oughtta get a award for the Most Asinine Lover of New York City. The one who gave and lost the most in this decade."

Cypress swung around the room, flinging her arms and kicking. All her movements were correct; sharp, and unexpected. Her anger pushed through her space. Idrina moved to another room, satisfied Cypress would let her legs scream out her disappointment.

Cypress fell down in the midst of furious *chené* turns. At first she wanted to jump up immediately and start again. A mad dance. A dance of expiation. A dance to exorcise Idrina and love and anything but movement. She wanted to get up and shout with her bosom and fingers. Holler with her arms: "I am hurt. I am hurt. I am hurt. HUUUURRRRRTTTT." But she didn't move;

she was rigid like a forsaken oak. Then she collapsed, refusing to dance—dance was too much joy to bear. She would not dance. She somehow got her things and left Idrina's in a fearsome silence. Cypress had nothing to say. No dance left.

My Darling Daughter,

Well Cypress, I am so glad you are studying so hard again. I was concerned while you were in California that you would do only the dances the Negroes have always done; all that jumping around and backside movement. I know you've never believed me, but it's on account of all that hip swinging that we colored women have such large rear ends. It has something to do with muscle development and gravity. That's all I know about it, but you remember what a hard time you had in the ballet . . . (smile). Anyway, if you keep going to classes that build up your technique, something good is bound to happen.

Your new friends, Idrina and Ixchell, sound very nice, but don't forget how I told all my girls that close women friends are always more trouble than they are pleasure. You can't ever keep your business to yourself, or be certain that your very own beau isn't the light of their life. Really, this is how women act. Seems we can't be true to anyone who isn't family.

So you be careful around all those women. Don't tell them too much. And don't introduce them to any of your fellas . . . 'less you want to learn the hard way. Remember

Mrs. Buchanan; well, she got to be Mrs. Buchanan by seducing her very best friend's fiancé during choir practice. That should be a lesson to you. Women will use you 'til you get some sense and keep to yourself, while being just as sociable and polite as a lady can be.

Sweetheart, you didn't mention whether you were taking any advanced ballet; I mean, do you still use your toe shoes? If you need some new ones, maybe I can contribute to that! Take real good care of yourself. Mind, you keep your distance from women with so little to do they stay around each other all the time, and pray that God'll see his way to placing you with a fine ballet company in New York City.

Lovingly,
Mama

U sually drinking made Cypress witty and lovey or terribly sleepy and lovey. Now it only made her quiet. And she drank all night, coming in as Celine and Ixchell were going to rehearsal. She slept all day. Around eight or nine she got up and dressed to go out drinking until the next day. She never said anything, not "how ya doin" or "see ya," she just stared and smiled to herself when someone spoke to her.

Cypress had discovered Harlem after-hours night life, and was becoming a regular at gambling spots and underworld taverns. Her refusal to speak and that smile drew "Outlaw Willie" and "Rolls-Royce Lou" to buy her drinks or some blow as a token for her madness. She didn't pick up anybody or make friends, she was just a regular. At an almost bar, two basements down, four bodyguards and five iron doors under an uptown tenement, another ex-dancer, Lily, did all of Cypress' talking for her. "She would like a Courvoisier, double." Nothing else was happening.

Before the Golden Onk opened up, Cypress made it to the downtown bars and pubs. Here, people she knew watched her uneasily, rarely spoke, but always noticed what she was drinking and that smile. She was in an old Irish tavern being taken over by Puerto Ricans and black artists on the Lower East Side, when she abruptly stopped making concentric circles in the sawdust under her feet, to listen. Cypress rushed toward the sound— music from home. She stood anxiously looking over shoulders in the back room, trying to see and share. Who was making this glory? Who was letting her speak? Cypress smiled and burst with "Yes. Yes. Yes." And before she remembered she didn't dance any more, she had leaped to the front of the musicians and was speaking of beauty and love in her body. Cypress danced her ass off, improvising and involving the audience in her joy. She whipped a shawl out of one woman's hand and a cigar out of an old fellow's mouth. With the lit end of the cigar in her mouth, the shawl over her head, Cypress moved as Yanvallou. Curved and low to the ground, her back undulated like Damballah's child must. The smoke eased from her mouth like holy vapor, pure and strong. The air was clean, the music rich. Cypress was dancing an old dance, a saxophone whispering hope all around her, love refusing to sit still. Cypress was a dance of a new thing, her own spirit loose, fecund, and deep.

As Leroy McCullough slipped the alto from his mouth, Cypress grabbed him and squeezed, and felt home again. Such a way to run into an old friend, while she was trying to be dead and silent. Leroy didn't know what was going on. Cypress wouldn't answer any of his questions about Sassafrass, or where she was living; she just got another drink and kept holding his hand, smiling and crying at the same time. When she blacked out in his arms, Leroy set her down in a back booth, went on with the next set, and carried her to his place. Cypress was smiling in her sleep.

Cypress was air. She felt so good. It was dark and someone was lying next to her. Someone's thigh, damp and heavy across her ass. She was warm; felt so good. She giggled, getting together where she was, who was this, why so good. Here she was herself again. She was her own mystery and this nice, wandering body was another thing to find out. Cypress crawled out from the legs and remembered Leroy. "Yes, this is Leroy. I was dancin' and this is Leroy."

Cypress ran her hands over his back, not a long back, but sturdy with wiry hairs growing up from the bottom. Thighs covered with masses of slight nappy curls, and funny calves like piano sticks with all the muscle bunched up near the knee. There was a mole on his right ankle. Some kind of birthmark where his ass rounded under. Cypress couldn't believe she was enjoying looking at a man, having such a good time. She turned him over softly, coaxing him.

"It's just me, Cypress."

And he went on sleeping and Cypress looked and kissed and giggled and touched. She sat over Leroy for ages, thinking about Idrina, fascinated with Leroy, wondering about herself.

He was so beautiful, and he woke up. They were silent, letting visions and nakedness speak. Leroy stared at Cypress the same way she had traced every line of his body. There was air. There was Roscoe Mitchell wild. There was Aramide, Halifu, all the dancers of the world. Energy between them was maddening. There were tongues and fingers, lips holding. As Leroy moved into her, Cypress plunged to the edge of the rainbow.

She left her address on the edge of a paper towel on the foot of the bed. It was day. It was time to dance, no matter what. . . .

157/

Ntozake Shange

braided lady of subway scents & magic
rings in nose & wrists/ music in the style of the islands
lacin the trains dancin in the tunnels of hades
ka-jungle-jingle-ka-jungle juju
in damp downtown nights of love/ the secrets of muscles
used
lights cajolin the tense spring of calves jumpin/ space
taken by the ripplin womanness of yr back/
do as you please/ african lady roamin los campos
of the lower east side/ caresses you with fried plantains
& drummers stealin corners for the winds to lift you
to the scant sun's ray/ lyric lady/ dance the original
dance
the original aboriginal dance of all time/ challenge the
contradiction of perfected pirouette with the sly knowin
of hips that do-right/ stretch till all the stars n sands
of all our lands abandoned/ mingle in the wet heat/
sweat & grow warm/ must be she the original
aboriginal dancin girl.

Leroy woke to a mass of hair that smelled so sweet from love he took a minute to realize it was his own. His hands swept across the bed—still damp—and he stretched out, waiting for her limbs to stop his. It was the truth; she was gone. He had to laugh; how could he get mad. If someone had pulled him dead drunk from anywhere and made love like some flock of wild scarlet birds, he'd probably have left as quietly as possible, too. "But no," he thought, "I wouldn't have gone without a taste more . . . something for the morning." Now that was good.

Cypress wasn't at all like her sister, and Leroy tried to remember if she really had arched backward over the bed so her pussy was at the foot and her head on the floor. Was it true that one leg wrapped all round his chest and the other thigh touched the ceiling? Yes, yes.

158/

He rubbed himself where his body remembered such carrying on, and he looked over the bed, placing Cypress in his arms, between his legs, under his chin, all over his hair . . . and he smelled his locks one more time, before he decided she'd be his. That made him feel so good he did one hundred push-ups, chanted his mantra, showered, and composed three variations of a theme called "When You Get Back Where You Can't Get Enough," before he went to rehearse his band, if you could call it that.

Leading a band of five or six cats who were near starving or living with women who were near starving, or who found time to play music in between getting the money for their dope, was not what Leroy wanted to do. He wanted a music that was a force, and to have that he'd have to have a bunch of cats who were force, full and clear.

But where were they? Where were they . . . shit, what a stupid question. They were all over the place just like he'd been—from one conservatory to another, one "jazz" ensemble to the next . . . white bands, black bands, orchestras, orquestras, arkestras. Leroy shook his head, remembering how hard it had been for him to hear what he heard. White folks kept telling him those sounds are impossible: "you *can't* do that to the piano" . . . "you *can't* push a saxophone that way" . . . "you *can't; you can't*" . . . "You should work on your Bach . . . Your Bartók needs more subtlety . . . You are rushing the Shostakovich . . . There's more to Prokofiev than you could imagine, my boy" . . . Every slight Leroy had endured in all those years piqued his skin. He thought he might be getting hives. They thought they were giving him credit when early Ellington and Henderson arrangements were offered as an elective for half a credit.

"Sheeit. My daddy grew up on that."

159/

Ntozake Shange

The patronizing reply: "Well, of course, but did he understand it?"

Leroy was sure he was getting hives. He focused on the day they turned down Ornette Coleman as a possible supervisor for independent study—Composition—but approved Steve Lacy, who wasn't even in the country. And even though he'd had to import a bunch of cats from New York for his graduate project because the white boys said it was impossible to "read" his notation system, even though he had graduated with honors because of the beauty of this Suite that was impossible to "read," his advisor's last words had been, "You don't need all that ethnic flourish, Leroy, you are too good to work in the Negro idiom." So the issue wasn't "where were they," the issue was how could they make it in a place like the Golden Onk.

It had been closed down three times for fire code violations, once for selling alcohol to minors, another time for being underneath the food code . . . beneath the food code, humph. They probably sold rat dung as a matter of course. Leroy felt the wall slide onto his back. Maybe Cypress didn't even remember how he loved her last night. Maybe she didn't even care.

"Cypress . . ." he sighed, running his fingers through the hair below his navel. Cypress liked women, or so the rumor went. Now the sister, Sassafrass, was the one who was into men and horns and babies; but everybody from Oakland to Fort Greene had heard that Cypress belonged to some bull-dyke cult, and the queen of Azure Bosom had laid right into whatever Cypress' trip had been.

"Dammit, shit. I sure do pick 'em." Leroy stomped his foot. Why hadn't it been Sassafrass? He designed ploys that Cypress had used against him. She had been so close to him to prove to herself that she was as much

160/

a woman as her sister, because that's when she had
warmed up to him, after recognizing him from that party
in San Francisco. Oh shit. That party had been in Cypress' house, and Sassafrass had been wandering around
like a new member of the Catatonic Virgin's Club. Why,
Cypress had even encouraged him to seek out her sister.

But here in New York, Cypress had been the one. She
had been too drunk to lie, too open to make believe all
night long. He was certain of that. Not all night long. Not
quite like that. Leroy packed up his horns and set off for
the Onk. A quick cognac and a good reed would be all
he needed until that hussy crossed his mind again. Then
he'd smell the scent of her on his moustache and wait.
She'd turn up.

From eight o'clock that morning until nine-thirty that
night Cypress was in and out of dance classes, from one
end of Manhattan to the other. Whatever she had
learned with that honey-lipped hornplayer was working
for her today. She had started out at Clark Center with
a morning ballet class that kicked her ass. She'd been
neglecting her technique in the freestyle Southern im-
provisations of The Kushites Returned & Company. At
the barre she smiled at all those pelvic muscles, hearing
her mama whispering that she had better work hard,
because the white folks didn't want to see a colored
woman fly of her own powers. She knew the muscles in
the top of her thighs were crying for relief, but between
a full night of Leroy and a morning of advanced interme-
diate, relief was out of the question.

Cypress was truly inspired. She moved like she had
never dared move on her own, without Ariel or Idrina
there to watch and give approval. She was free of something that had been holding her back, something that set
limits to what she could do, how she could move. She

felt so much the diva she decided that for the rest of the day she'd wear her red leotard with the embroidery round her backside and up her crotch. That's the one she'd take her place in, and the first teacher who called her out, saying, "If you are going to look like that, Miss, I hope you can dance like that," would get such a performance from her that she'd be asked to join a company immediately. And if she joined a company, she could stay in New York with Leroy. But Leroy didn't know she wanted to stay. And she hadn't known she wanted to stay with him. She was working herself into a panic, when she heard a voice she knew too well.

"Listen, girl, I'm telling you Lilah James, Eleo Pomare, Rod Rodgers, Royal Brown, Sounds-In-Motion all gonna be in this special gala for that grand lady of black dance, Savilla Forte. Plus the Dance Theatre of Harlem, Ailey's Junior Company, and us, Azure Bosom."

"You serious?"

"Would I lie to you about our coming of age, our first real break in the City?"

"Oh, Idrina, that's so wonderful. I'm so happy for you. I guess I got back just in time to see my lady strut 'cross that stage."

Cypress moved to throw her dance clothes in her bag and run. She didn't. She told each muscle that had frozen, every gland that was sweating and joint that ached, to let go, to just let go. Laura and Idrina, just beyond the dressing room, talked like they were the very last lovers on the planet. Cypress fixed her mouth to shout, but didn't. She simply nodded. Yes, today was the day for the red leotard with the embroidery, the yellow leg warmers, the rhinestone waistband, and the best series of turns she'd ever accomplished. Maybe six pirouettes would do, for today. With a grand *jeté* just over Idrina's head.

"Yeah. Idrina never gave me credit for all I could do." Cypress stretched once and sauntered toward the laughter of two women who weren't thinking about her.

Laura looked nothing like Cypress had figured. She didn't look like she lived in Manhattan, or had even ever been in Manhattan. Cypress forced herself to see this Laura with Idrina, among the other women from Azure Bosom. Women with lavender hair, nose rings, toe rings, and passions of sub-Saharan Sapphos. She had to put her hand over her mouth to hide the grin. Laura was all of four-foot-ten. Innocent as a child raised in a convent a hundred years ago. Soft like the bubbles of a bath of rose damask. Not one line of malice edged her eyes, there was no permanent pout in her lower lip. Her only extravagance was the placement of five diamond studs around her left ear, so her female orifices sparkled no matter what time of day, no matter who could see. But these thoughts had to hurry along, because now Cypress had to speak to this Laura before this moment of glory, or mischief, passed by.

Leaning against the lockers in the hallway, hips pushed forward like she might give birth, Idrina shouted, "Why Cypress, it's so good to see you!" She pulled up to hug Cypress, so close their nipples almost touched. Then the two, Cypress and Idrina, grabbed each other. Laura watched Idrina in this warm reunion, knowing that Cypress was looking her straight in the face, as if to say, "Now what?" There was a silence that any one of them could have broken, and Laura said:

"Hi, Cypress, I'm Laura. I've been waiting to meet you."

Idrina pulled back as the two women spoke. Cypress, feeling ebullient from the night before with Leroy, thought she'd take it all, and cooed,

"Oh, not nearly as long as I've wanted to meet you."

Idrina jumped in with an idea that they should go celebrate her company's good fortune.

For some reason Cypress thought about her mother in Carolina, weaving away whole years of her life, but not losing control of any. She saw her mama over the stove, going on about the kind of place New York was and why she'd never go there . . . but she trusted the Lord to look after her dancing daughter in that hellified place where sin and temptation whet every appetite. Cypress hoped she was thinking loud enough for her mama to hear, "Well, Ma, we're in New York now," but her mother was still over the stove and had no useful information concerning social amenities in this situation. Cypress choked a desperate laugh that caused Laura and Idrina to jump back and ask what was wrong. Cypress swallowed a little, and fighting tears ready to reveal her innocence, not her worldliness, said, "Oh, nothing." Still, she asked herself what her mama would do, now . . . only to hear her mama's voice saying, "No girl. I don't know what you're doing."

They made off for a Greek restaurant near 48th Street, Laura in the middle, Cypress and Idrina catching glimpses of one another over Laura's head. A tense gaiety enveloped them. Cypress examined Laura, taking her apart gesture by gesture, limb by limb; the way her tongue fell through the tiny gap in her front teeth, while the diamonds shone on Idrina. Then before she knew exactly what she was doing, Cypress stopped, softly touched Laura's shoulder, caught Idrina's attention, pulled her dance bag closer to her and said:

"I've got a twelve o'clock jazz class way uptown. I had better catch the train."

Laura didn't seem to believe what Cypress was saying . . . "Oh, no . . . !", and Cypress, laid back on her right hip, retorted,

"Oh, yes. 'Cause I'm gonna be someone to reckon with around here, sometime, so I got to go to class. Right, Idrina?"

All Idrina could bring herself to say was, "Uh huh, but are you gonna come to the concert tonight? It'll be the first time that Azure Bosom has ever appeared before mixed audiences, you know."

Cypress threw out an "Of course," and was gone. Erzulie always thought she was cute.

Not much was on her mind except catching the A train, and getting rid of images of Laura and Idrina curled up on each other in a nostalgic twilight, but she thought hard again, trying to make her mama feel her gratitude.

"Mama, you lied. You knew just what to do. Don't break bread with folks you can't trust."

That's all it took. Imagine sharing dalma and lamb with Laura and Idrina. No, no, not in this life. Cypress wished Sassafrass and Indigo could be with her on Eighth Avenue. They could sing like Martha and the Vandellas to "Come and Get These Memories," the sound of their voices on megaphones from Times Square to Columbus Circle. They weren't there, so Cypress sang alone. People on the street thought she was a jackleg panhandler.

"No, no. Take your money back. I'm doing this for free."

JOURNAL ENTRY #298

whatchu cant have you just cant have
who aint meant just aint in you
who be gone just aint there
what aint yrs/ must be somebody else's
you gotta bring what you be needin

you gotta unwind-wound-down/ take a look a round
& bring what you be needin

The Golden Onk had never looked so bad. Cypress
was sober enough to see the years of dirt mixed with
current grime, the elbow spots worn into the bar from
night after night of heavy drinkers, the odor of old
anything akin to whiskey, folks who stayed too long in
the same pair of drawers. What Leroy was doing in this
hellhole confounded her. So far only a couple of neighborhood junkies had wandered in from Avenue A. Four
nasty-looking beatnik types were reminiscing in the far
corner. Cypress had sized up the bartender as one of
those whimsical black guys committed to integration at
any cost. That was the reason he hadn't paid her too
much mind: she didn't advance the cause of race relations.

One peach brandy down and one fine nigger coming
up, or so she hoped. Leroy would appear in a second to
break down the instruments, and she could tell him
about everything she'd seen since she left his place. Two
black beauties on the corner of 49th and 8th. Four
raving queens in crocheted bikinis, 59th Street station.
Six perfect sets of nails from 96th to 145th Street. One
free colored gal in a red leotard soaring through the
skies. One dancer who couldn't forget the second night
that changed her life.

J O U R N A L   E N T R Y   #692:

what does it mean that blk folks cd sing n dance?
why do we say that so much/ we dont know what we
mean/
i saw what that means/ good god/ did i see/ like i
cda

166/

*walked on the water myself/ i cda clothed the naked
& fed
the hungry/ with what dance i saw tonite/ i don't
mean dance
i mean a closer walk with thee/ a race thru swamps
that fall
off in space/ i mean i saw the black people move the
ground
& set stars beneath they feet/ so what's this mean
that
black folks cd dance/ well/ how abt a woman like
dyane harvey who can make
her body the night riders & the runaways/ the
children hangin
on they mama's dress/ while they father's beat to
death/ the
blood/ from the man's wounds/ his woman's tears/
the night riders
goin off in darkness/ the silence of the night*

*how abt bernadine j. whose body waz all of that in
5 minutes/ & whose very presence humbled all but
the drum/
now that's a dance/ like rael lamb careenin cross
the stage on his bare stomach/ fifty feet/
sounds like possums n rattlesnakes/ mississippi
undercurrents
& steamin hog mawls/ tossin him from decatur to
south texas/
tearin him from contraction to leaps so expansive/
his body
took the space allowed thirty redwood trees/ & those
sounds
kept pushin him/ little racing motors like the cops
waz*

round the bend/ windows opened & shut cuz there
are things
others ought not hear/ feet on stairways of burned
out homes/
the sounds pushed him/ & there was a dance that
was a black
dance/ that's what it means that black folks cd
dance/ it
dont mean we got rhythm/ it dont mean the slop or
the hully gully/
or this dance in houston callt "the white boy"/ it
dont mean just
what we do all the time/ it's how we remember what
cannot be said/
that's why the white folks say it aint got no form/
what was the form
of slavery/ what was the form of jim crow/ & how
wd they
know . . .

That a kiss on the third vertebra down from the nape of
her neck would make Cypress hum . . . a dance she
would do with Leroy that night and many nights to come;
a dance that began without a word of explanation, no
questions, nothing hard, except the empty seats by the
bar. The bite of cheap whiskey made sweet, as Leroy's
hands flew under her skirt to the edge of her clit, saying
"Do you want me" when he could . . . because he
couldn't keep talking with his tongue in her ear, behind
her ear, biting her scalp above her eye. And every time
he said anything he'd move his fingers over the rose-red
vulva, with Cypress wanting exactly where those fingers
just left. He'd sigh, "How much," and Cypress could feel
lightning in her back, and he'd say, "That's not
enough," and she thought, "Jesus, the man has no

mercy." But she was too glad to care about mercy; if she and this man could turn the Golden Onk into a sure enough Paradise, who'd take the time to tell them the bar was closing?

Cypress sat up slowly so she wouldn't disturb Leroy, who was sleeping the sleep of an old tortoise on a deserted beach. She pulled her shoulders toward the wall, lifting his head over her legs, laying his face on her thigh, leaving his locks in a great fan from her knee to the fold in her hip where so much fire had leaped between them. There were too many things she wanted to do, all at once. To run her finger over her lips to rekindle where those sleeping lips had driven her to abandon; to figure if Leroy was simply perfect . . . or perverse; like he was sleeping now, like all he needed, he had. That nothing bothered him, because everything was fine.

"I wouldn't believe any of it, if it hadn't been me. I mean if I hadn't been there, I'd say I was lyin.' " Cypress spoke softly while she curled the long braids round her wrists. "I guess I could be insulted . . . maybe I should be outraged." She went on, now that she could put the last few days in some order. She liked to make lists: lists of what happened to her; lists of who loved her; lists of who hurt her; lists of things to wear; lists of surprises, and her time with Leroy was replete with surprises.

S U R P R I S E   #1

When they left the Golden Onk that night she'd fallen off the barstool from too much finger fucking. Leroy had given her a piggyback ride to Fifth Avenue, before he asked, "Girl, don't you have any clothes or personal belongings?" Cypress jumped off his back, remembering all her marvelous Chinese silks, her kaftans and silk stockings with seams, the combs of sea shells and feathers, her satin slips and camisoles. She wanted to scream "What kind of woman do you think I am," but she realized she'd been in the same peasant skirt (the blue one with roses and violets) and a yellow Mexican blouse with lace on the sleeves ever since she'd left Idrina's. Now she did wash it out on occasion, but that had been a while, too. Was Leroy saying she was dirty? Was this one of those times to weep for forgiveness, or was this a time to have a shocked faint? Cypress looked somewhere other than directly at Leroy or herself, though she covered her bosom like a thirteen-year-old who'd gotten her period at the movies.

"They're in a bunch of lockers at the East Side Terminal. No, that's not true. They're on the 9th Avenue side of Port Authority."

"Okay then. Let's go."

"Go where?"

"To get the runaway's things."

"Well, where am I gonna take 'em?"

"You don't have any sense of romance, do you? No stars in your eyes or sensations of magic, humph?"

Cypress saw the Empire State Building do a slow drag at that very moment. She thought there were lilac trees on the corners of 9th Avenue and 14th Street. The meat-packing houses turned into aquariums for giant fishes the colors of sunset in Puerto Rico. She was being taken home; she was finally going to her house in New York. When they'd lined up all her boxes and baskets of things from her closets in California, Leroy just smiled at her.

"Can ya carry all of these parcels on your head the way the women in Haiti do?"

Cypress tried because she wanted so much for Leroy's every dream of her to be true, but when the fourth attempt failed, they took a cab to the loft.

SURPRISE #2

One day she was improvising in the mirror while getting dressed, so that each movement was the reverse of a strip-tease, because she was putting on more and more things. And Leroy would hand her strange objects: a box of hominy grits, *Jet* magazine, or Nadinola skin cream . . . they were dressing her at an incredible pace. Finally she took on the stance of a tango, with a mass of feather combs streaming from her mouth. This had been Leroy's idea, and now he sat just beneath her, feeling her calf.

"You know sometimes, not very often, but sometimes, you move like Idrina. Did you know that?"

All the play stopped. Cypress dropped to the floor in front of Leroy, who took the feathers out of her mouth and kissed her quickly, like "I-love-you-but-we-have-to-talk" kisses can be. With his hands under her chin, he said again, "Did you know that, that you move like her?" Cypress saw herself in the Mojave Desert; stranded homeless, loverless. She saw Azure Bosom take her in and care for her. She did not believe Leroy was trying to get her to renounce Idrina, or the other women she danced with who loved her, the other women who knew that womanhood was as sacred a right as liberty. Her eyes were those of a she-wolf, while her body still lingered for him like a gazelle's.

"Oh, that's not surprising. We worked together for a long time when I first came here. I admire Idrina."

Leroy got up, and walked to the windows. He saw Idrina straddled 'cross the tower of the Empire State

Building, legs pushing through clouds, and women floating around her mouth like gulls by the Santa Monica
pier. He looked harder, and made the skyline a thousand
beds for the French girls who always came in pairs
. . . it was more fun that way, they'd say. Then by trial
and error he'd have to keep tasting to see which one had
the coke on her pussy and which one didn't. He knew
Cypress didn't belong out there in the sky with the
women he remembered, conjured from other days. Yet
she had been among them, flung from wing to breast, to
tongue, to flight. Would she want that again, a world
where he could not be seen? Leroy was too much of a
gentleman to reveal the depth of his need for Cypress to
want to stay. He'd resisted this kind of closeness ever
since his parents died. Cypress might be his chance for
true intimacy, but she'd shared so much with so many;
while he took as little as possible, gave what could be
spared without having to remember. With his back to
Cypress, he didn't see how beautiful she looked in the
mirrors; how there were three illusions of her, with the
fleshbound Cypress on the floor amidst hominy, feathers, and cloth . . . and more illusions.

"I know all that Cypress. I live with you. I've lived
in New York for the past eight years. I know who Idrina
is."

Cypress looked at herself in one mirror, then the
others. She could see that there was something enticing
about her ensemble of kitchenware and petticoats, but
there was also something distorted. Was it that Leroy
wasn't saying what he really wanted to say? There was
a half-truth hovering; some vestiges of a lie were over-
taking them. "Well, I thought I loved her."

"You did or you thought you did?" Leroy queried as
he turned toward her, because now there were no secrets
being kept, no reason to walk away. Cypress was going

to be honest, he hoped. He would have prayed she'd be honest, but he didn't want to give her any help. She had to do it on her own.

"Well, you loved the woman or you didn't, which was it?"

Cypress didn't like being put on the spot. She didn't like having to answer for her own time, her own feelings, her choices.

"Is it your business what I was doing before I met you?"

"No, but it's my business what you're doing now."

"What are you talking about?"

"Boy, you think the world's got the memory of a fool. Don't you think I know why you were drinking yourself silly in bar after bar for weeks when Laura came back? Don't you think I know why you haven't mentioned your great admiration for Idrina before?"

"No, why don't you tell me."

"Oh, Cypress. I'm not attacking you. I just wanna talk to you; I wanna know you're here 'cause you want ta be, not 'cause you're runnin' away from somebody. Is that so hard to understand?" Leroy moved over to where Cypress was idly undoing her peculiar array. "Listen, I want you. I don't care what you did before, I'm just not sure you've finished with her, that's all." He slipped his arms over her shoulders, and pulled her up to him. "I think it's wonderful for two women to be lovers, there's a sanctity to it that I respect. And I'm glad for you to have known all that is, but, Cypress, you can't dress it up, or cheapen it down, by saying you 'thought' you loved her, see what I mean?"

Cypress relaxed in Leroy's grasp, fell closer to his body, smelled that smell of his that reminded her of coffee and the sea. She opened her mouth, let her tongue glide over his collarbone, whispering, "I did love her. I still love her, Leroy, like one of my sisters." Leroy took a deep breath, inhaled all the air he could and poked Cypress repeatedly with his inflated stomach, like an Americanized Yanvallou. It was only seconds before she realized he'd chased her back to their bed; only a few more seconds before they were no more than shout and sweat, and released. Cypress was gone; absolutely dead to the world. Leroy caught himself whispering, "I know it's terrible. I shouldn't have done it. You can't fuck somebody into loving you, but I had to, I had to. She can't leave me for that bitch, she can't. I won't allow it."

Now she was awake and he was asleep. Cypress decided that she could sleep too, because all she needed, she had. Nothing bothered her, because everything was fine. If they ever got up she was going to cook a meal that all Carolina would envy.

CYPRESS' MEAL
FOR MANHATTAN NIGHTS

Barbequed Lamb Manhattan

3–4 pound leg of lamb
¾ cup blackstrap molasses
2 cans tomato sauce
2 stalks celery, cubed
1 medium onion, diced
1 green pepper, diced

1 lemon, quartered
2 teaspoons chili powder
1 teaspoon hot dry mustard
Dash of Worcestershire
Red pepper, salt, black
   pepper to taste

Score lamb crossways, one inch deep & one inch apart. Boil remaining ingredients for barbeque sauce. Marinate the lamb with ½ of your sauce for about 45 minutes, then place lamb in roasting pan in 300° oven for 1½ to 2 hours, basting every 15 minutes.

Nighttime Potato Salad/ 'Cuz There's No Time to Cool

6 good-sized potatoes
3 hard-boiled eggs
1 onion, diced
1 stalk celery, diced
3 tablespoons prepared sweet
relish

½ teaspoon dry mustard
1 cup mayonnaise
Salt & pepper to taste
Paprika to sprinkle over top

Boil potatoes till tender. With old-fashioned potato masher, break into smaller chunks in mixing bowl. Chop eggs, celery, onion & add to potatoes, along with the other ingredients. Mix well. Check to see if it's too dry. If so, add a little more mayonnaise. Sprinkle paprika over the finished salad. Serve.

Easy Asparagus

½ pound baby asparagus
(16)

1 lemon
¼ teaspoon powdered ginger

Wash asparagus. Slice off bad ends if they are tough or brown. Sprinkle ginger over the asparagus. Squeeze lemon over the asparagus. Chill and serve.

Cypress dear,

Where you're living sounds so wonderful, but I'm not sure I understand what a loft is, exactly. Is it just a big room, or something more special? Then too, you musn't brag about how much you'll get for something later. You shouldn't let everyone know how much store you set by something . . . and I definitely believe you should speak with your landlord about this fixture fee business—sounds crooked to me. Who ever heard of paying for a toilet and tub . . . in decent lodgings the management always supplies such. I know New York is different and that you've more experience with some things than I have, but mark my words. Somebody's gypping you.

If it's just a big room, how did you manage to have a duplex living quarters? I guess I can't quite imagine seeing the Hudson River and New Jersey from one window and walking 'cross a floor to see the Empire State Building. Is Macy's big enough to see from where you live? I've wanted to go to Macy's ever since <u>Miracle on 34th Street</u>. Let me know, will you?

I'm not going to go on about your relationship with this young man. You and Sassafrass will have to discover on your own that there's no kind of man that takes seriously what comes too easy. From his picture he seems to have nice features, a well-bred looking sort, but my goodness how could you lay your head on the same pillow with that mess he calls hair on his head? Artist or not, that boy's got to cut his hair. Then you could bring him home for a holiday, but don't bring him down here looking like he looks. It'll set the race back a hundred years.

I think I recall Sassafrass mentioning this Leroy to me before. Is he a friend from California? From what you say, he doesn't sound at all like that Mitch poor Sassafrass is tied to; I hope he's not, for your sake. But she does carry herself a little different from you, Cypress. I'm not meaning to find fault, but you've always got to keep a little money of your own somewhere, because men come and go like the weather. It's not respectable for a young woman to be totally beholdin to any young man, especially if she's not married. In my day, there were names for those women and I didn't raise you to be one of them. You continue to go to those auditions. Get yourself in a company and see if your "perfect" young man doesn't improve as much as a "perfect" young man could. (smile)

Oh, I nearly forgot. Thank you so much for that kimona. The silk is so fine, I feel downright sinful when I wear it. Of course, no one's here to see me in it, but I do think your father might have come home more often, if I'd had one of these.

Much love to you,
Mama

P.S. Don't forget to have that boy cut that mess off his head —he'll thank you for it later, when he doesn't look such a fool.

*C*ypress hated the walk home from a Friday class. There were too many people in too much hurry. Things didn't smell good after a week of wage-slavery. Folks looked stale and dishevelled until they accepted the weekend as a reality. Maybe she was being too hard on the general public. Maybe she was the one who was worn out from a week of hard physical labor. If that was the case, she deserved some treats. And treat herself grandly is what she did. Any boutique or vegetable stand worth looking at from Greenwich Avenue to Waverly Place, she graced with her consumer dollar: artichokes; leotards; silk scarves; barrettes; asparagus; Port Salut cheese; two bottles of La Doucette because Leroy liked that; and an honest-to-god laced corset like the ones in the nasty movies where men fantasize nasty things, or so she imagined. With these delicacies and this corset over her body smelling of almonds, she'd have her way with that insanely perfect man she lived with.

It annoyed her sense of anarchy, the way he worked. From seven in the morning until one, he practiced. Then from one o'clock until three he composed. Around four he'd meet somebody for a rehearsal or keep writing music. He did this every day, even Sunday. Cypress thought that was a bit much. He made her feel like she was lazy. Yet he never criticized her use of time. She got up with him and did her hieroglyphs in needlepoint to ease her mind and soothe her ancestors, then she was off to the dance studio of her choice for class until early evening.

"No, I guess I'm not lazy," Cypress consoled herself. "Hey, wait a minute . . ." Stopping herself in front of Balducci's with her bags of exotic vegetables, wines, and feminine apparel. "What the fuck are we living on?" Cypress was down to her last $750.00. That was all that was left from the stash she'd brought from California. Dealing coke in New York was out of the question; she had no connections, no customers, no protection.

"Oh, Jesus, he's a dope dealer or something, a gun-runner. Who in the hell knows. Oh shit, what am I gonna do, say 'Leroy, do you mind if I take a lil of your trade?' What kind of mess am I in now. I let him give me the money and I never asked where it came from. I'm such a jackass."

The wonderful bundles lost their favored status. Cypress walked toward the loft with the air of some demented bag-lady, who'd just been pushed off her corner.

Just as she thought. Leroy was still composing music, right on schedule.

"You know, you're too predictable, Leroy," she hollered in the quiet. Leroy realized Cypress must have had a very bad day to behave in such a manner first thing. He didn't pick up on the querulous tones in her voice, but let them go right on by.

"Cypress, what's the matter with you?" he said, without looking up from his work. Cypress stood still, holding her luscious treats specially chosen to seduce this man who wasn't looking at her. She felt like she was three, and there was going to be no Sunday picnic, no swings, no watermelon. When Leroy took a glance at her, he burst out laughing.

"Look Cypress, whatever it is, come on out with it! Have you hurt yourself, or did one of your 'marvelous' teachers find you out of form?" Cypress started to cry, slow little girl tears, so her face stayed smooth and glowing.

"What do we live on, Leroy? How do we live here?"

Leroy seemed puzzled. "Well, I pay the bills and I give you money that you need to go to class, or whatever you want . . . I think . . . that's all there is to it."

Cypress slammed her fist on Leroy's desk. "No that's not what I mean. I mean where does the money come from? We don't work. No—I know we work, but we don't earn any money. We don't have money to pay for a place like this, or my classes, or all this stuff I bought today."

Leroy really thought she was funny, now. "Yes we do, honey, and there's more where that came from."

Cypress, totally befuddled, sat on Leroy's lap while he whistled one of his tunes to her. The tune that meant there was nothing to fear. More than niggers could burn, more than blues and fury, found a voice in Leroy.

"Cypress, do you think you could hum 'Air Above Mountains'? . . . Well, alright, let's do a duet of 'Theme of the Yoyo,' the Art Ensemble's soundtrack with Fontella Bass. I know you know it."

Cypress said nothing.

"You think I might be doing something outside the law, huh? You think you might be in some mess like Sassafrass and that junkie of hers, don't you?"

Cypress didn't want to say, "Yes, that's what I thought," but she shook her head, yes, that's what she thought.

"Wow, Cypress, do you think I'd be as good as you in a business like that?" Leroy had to rock her so she'd calm down, but she kept wrestling with him until he swore, "I'll show you where the money comes from, okay?"

"Is it dangerous?"

"No darling, it's benign."

Cypress and Leroy followed the maitre d' to a table for four by the windows of one of those restaurants advertised in the "Preferred" section of tourist magazines. What they were doing in a place like this was beyond her. It was just like being on the road, searching for a meal that wasn't Howard Johnson's Americana or terribly prepared French cuisine adapted to American tastes, available in the "better" hotels. Cypress kept looking around to see who was going to join them, but all she could set her eyes on was lace: 1/2 leno alternating with 2/1 leno; allover 2/2 Mexican lace in one, in ivory, natural cotton.

"My oh my, how they want us to know this is frequented by genteel society." Lace table cloths, lace curtains . . . yes, Cypress checked, lace borders on the napkins. "Oh these poor people," Cypress thought, "these poor people would never imagine that I grew up in all this goddamned lace. I've spent my life getting out of lace-y places."

And the French accents grated, rather than soothed her. After all, foreign white folks were just as indisposed to the colored as American ones. But foreigners could be more dangerous, if you didn't understand what they were saying. Yet this was where Leroy's business was to be made clear to her.

Cypress had, to her mind, dressed for the occasion. Her shoulders lay bare under the thinnest of satin straps; the blouse fell over her bosom, sensually peach.

Ntozake Shange

Huge lime flowers that had never been seen on earth spread over the deep blue of her crepe skirt. Her eyes were shaded in greens, her lashes aqua. Lips, blackberry and ripe. Her hair flew about her head in wafts held with ebony combs.

Between nibbles of peppercorn pâté and sips of Charbaut et Fils champagne, she slipped coyly into the role of the Southern belle being courted by a Northern industrialist. Cypress preened, blushed, giggled, and delighted Leroy with her antics: Tallulah at dinner; Zelda after cocktails; Miz Fitzhugh with an aperitif. What held her series of caricatures together was her expert use of a white laced hankie that her mother had given her. This hankie spun in the air, as Leroy and Cypress played damsel and gallant.

Cypress was just about to describe the antics of po' white trash in Carolina when she noticed the maitre d' showing a couple to their table. In a grey linen suit and ivory silk blouse with her initials on the collar, the woman carried a bone leather clutch-purse. Her hair was straightened by one of those permanents that never turn back—makeup straight out of *Cosmo*. The man was in an openweave beige jacket, with a flamingo shirt that opened easily at the neck. His shoulders were broad and highlighted by the startlingly white cravat that fell beneath his lapels. Cypress squirmed, trying not to make a face.

"Oh no, not all night, not with them," she thought. "Enter the Black Bourgeoisie, the Talented Tenth and all that," turning to Leroy to save her. But Leroy was obviously excited to see these two. Everybody was glad to see everyone. Cypress was the loner. Leroy stood, to kiss the woman on her cheek.

"Cypress, this is Mahlon Burbridge, and Towbin Owens; old classmates of mine."

182/

Cypress could tell from the way Mahlon shook hands
that the girl hadn't been raised properly. There was no
force to the grip, no energy. Lord help women who shook
hands like dead fish. Don't they know their handshakes
are a sign of the verity of their word; if you can't shake
hands, you can't be trusted. "No backbone," she could
hear her mama say. But Mahlon smiled warmly, so Cypress did her best to put off making a judgment so early
in the evening.

Now, Towbin Owens was a different matter. His hand-
shake held authority, as did his voice. Everything about
Towbin Owens was all right with Cypress. She looked
back and forth from Leroy to Tobin, because they were
so alike in a way, yet so different. While Leroy was the
more refined of the two—even with his dreadlocks and
casual attire—Tobin's irrepressible enthusiasm comple-
mented his formal demeanor.

Once they were all seated, Cypress and Mahlon fell
into conversation.

"So Towbin tells me you're an artist, too."

"Yes, a dancer."

"I've always wanted to be an artist, but I guess I don't
have any talents, that way."

Cypress had been waiting for this. The moment when
the nice girl who did what mama had told her to do
would begin to wish and want that she had not done what
her mama told her. Cypress asked quite genuinely:

"Well, what did you end up doing with the talents you
do have?"

"I'm a stockbroker."

Cypress didn't know what to say. She couldn't say,
"Oh that's too bad, you Capitalist Pig," because this was
Leroy's friend. "Do you deal in napalm after six?"
would be too caustic, and, "Tell me, does money actually
burn up in niggahs' hands?" would be too familiar. So

Cypress didn't say anything but "How nice for you."

Cypress was giving Leroy the "rescue-me" eye, when her food arrived. Duck baked in black cherries with brandy, wild rice, string beans with almonds. Leroy was having poached salmon with garnished potatoes; Mahlon and Towbin were sharing a rack of lamb, medium rare. "Thank God," Cypress sighed to herself, now Leroy could handle the repartee. Cypress didn't want to talk to Mahlon alone any more; she wanted this duck, and more cherry sauce.

Apparently, Leroy, Mahlon, and Towbin had all gone to some experimental prep school in New England, Mahlon and Towbin on scholarships, Leroy by grace of his father's fortune. Even now, Mahlon looked at Leroy with the kind of awe that translates: "How could *he* exist, in the U.S.A." But the death of Leroy's parents (by local lore, an act of the Mafia; according to the insurance companies, an act of God), had left Leroy the sole survivor of his family. As they recounted their pasts to Cypress, Leroy said little. Mahlon was determined that Cypress understand.

"You see, as an eighteen-year-old, Leroy had control of his property in the state of Missouri, so Towbin advised Leroy to invest the money from the sale of the house and the insurance. He was our first client, and we've been looking after him ever since."

"Oh my," Cypress thought silently, "the Whiz Kids. No wonder Leroy never mentions family. He doesn't have any damn family." She glanced at Leroy. Now he'd explained where this money they lived on came from, but he hadn't explained so much else . . . no mention of this school, his parents, his loneliness and anger after such a thing.

Dr. McCullough and his wife Eleanora had been found burned to death in their car, on the way back to

St. Louis from the family farm south of Independence. Officially, the brakes failed. Leroy winced, as Towbin laid out the details.

"We think Dr. McCullough had been set up by organized crime, since he was running a successful campaign against gambling and vice in East St. Louis." Leroy waited for Towbin to say more. The two friends stared at each other; Towbin dropped his eyes first.

"Why don't you tell Cypress the rest," Leroy demanded.

"Leroy, you on that again? That was vicious hearsay, man. Let it be."

"No. Cypress, besides championing the rights of the decent citizen, they say my father had taken up with some white woman who was none other than the sister of some cracker in the rackets."

Leroy swallowed some cognac, and looked about absently. Towbin was exasperated.

"Listen, Leroy. All that was talk, man, just talk. Of course, they couldn't let a niggah die without spoiling his reputation. Another fool dying for a white woman, that's what they'd like us to think; but I knew your folks, Leroy, and you know that's not what happened."

"So you see, Cypress, according to the school therapists—or one of them—my father's adventures killed my mother and left me a wealthy orphan. Is that Oedipal enough for you?"

Cypress didn't know who to believe. Leroy had never expressed any hostility toward anybody as long as she'd known him, but now he was verging on bitterness. Mahlon caught Cypress' attention.

"I'm sorry this is happening, but each time Leroy sees us, he re-examines his parents' death. We were all together when the news came. Leroy's convinced his father sent him to Mountain Trust in order to protect him.

Sometimes he thinks he was sent away because his father could feel something about the danger they were in. But he knows better."

Towbin flashed on the twenty-eight of them, the colored kids. The Experiment in International Living, they'd called themselves. Twenty-eight out of nine hundred. And they were supposed to be in heaven, lolling about New England with the blue-bloods. Mountain Trust was never the same after them. Them, the Other. Who wore their ties under their turtlenecks, so the mentors would have to touch their varied skins. Them, in tennis shoes at chapel. Them, demanding invitations to public schools for socials so they would meet some folks who'd been colored all their lives and didn't have to talk about "how does it feel?" Mahlon, Leroy, and Towbin guarding their table in the dining hall, lest some good samaritan white kid sat down wanting to expand his or her cultural horizons. Black kids living in a socialist dream world that cost upwards of $4,000.00 a year. All of them raised a ruckus when they learned they had to work in potato fields and tend animals, even though they were on scholarship, everybody except Leroy and some of the Africans. Even so, what the fuck did they have to milk cows for, or paint barns. Towbin recalled saying, "Sheeeit, muthafuckah, I'll go to town and get you some goddamn milk." That was before the solitude seduced them, and let them have the right to struggle with the land. Thoughts they had no rights to be anywhere they chose, blew away with the coming of winter, until that day the telegram about Leroy's folks had arrived.

"Towbin," Leroy called out, "stop whispering to Cypress."

"We weren't whispering, man, I was giving her background information."

"Oh, my background. I come from a long line of civil

rights activist doctors and preachers, who have always managed to get killed at home, never while fighting for their country . . ."

Towbin could stand no more, and with all his authority ended Leroy's flippant histrionics. Cypress wanted to hug Leroy up close to her; rub away the mean lines that had grown across his forehead. He looked toward her, like she might leave him too, the way his parents did— without a word, in the middle of the night. She smiled to let him know that he was still the most perfectly perverse man she knew; the man she loved.

Leroy and Towbin eased over the past into current business and varieties of cognac: Courvoisier, Hennessey, V.S.O.P., Remy Martin. Towbin had left Mountain Trust to go on to Harvard, then Yale Law. Like Mahlon, he'd grown to be Leroy's family. And like family, there was pain between them. Cypress was relieved to talk with Mahlon now. She was the only other person not emotionally overwhelmed by the history of Leroy McCullough. Through all the evening's revelations, Mahlon became more tender, less severe than at first. Cypress wanted to tell her that, strange as it was, her father had died in a fire at sea. She was sure Leroy should have been the one to hear her say, years ago, that loss is not a crime, nor death a vendetta.

Every time her father went to sea, she and her sisters and her mama would wait, hoping he'd come back the way he left: with all his limbs, the quick gullah accent, how he'd laugh when he saw all three of them waiting for him on the stairway, peeking over the bannister to see Daddy. But one time he didn't come. One time there just was no more daddy but what you could remember, what you could make up in yourself that would be like him. That's why Cypress didn't mind travelling all the time, doing without a home of her own when she had to, collecting odds and ends from round the world, because that's what her father would have done. Maybe she was a dancer because her father couldn't stand being still.

Mahlon liked Cypress. Even though she was quiet, her body reflected anything she might say. So this was a dancer. Someone whose body interpreted the world. Mahlon felt her mouth draw tight around her teeth. Where she worked, there might not be anyone who moved more than their bowels. If she wore a bright color, the office workers stared at her all day. In the stacks at Columbia, she was always mistaken for the cleaning woman. At Bryn Mawr, they asked for their laundry. Even this afternoon, her secretary had gone on and on about how tragic it must be for her to be so educated when the "Negroes" were so far behind. Mahlon wanted to take the bitch to Chicago, leave her stranded on the South Side somewhere after two A.M. ... but Towbin had other ideas for the rest of the night.

"Let's catch the last set at the Vanguard. I think Betty Carter is there."

"No, man, Cypress and I are gonna turn in; artists don't have any days off, you know."

Leroy, back to his gentle self, pinched Cypress' legs under the table. Cypress, who'd been engrossed in talk with Mahlon about the black people in prep schools, turned to catch Leroy's hands.

"You could have told me."

Shaken from his jocular mood, Leroy very seriously asked, "Really, Cypress? I could have told you what? When was the last time you met a rich little colored boy?"

"Why last month I had a taxi driver from Nigeria who was to inherit oil and a noble title!"

"No, I'm not kidding, Cypress. What do you think would happen to me, if everybody knew?"

"Why, nothing. A lot of people care about you."

Towbin and Mahlon were leaving; hugs and kisses, promises to stay in touch interrupted Leroy's thoughts. He had to find a way to tell Cypress that he had to be as full a man as his father had been. He worked like he did because he knew that somehow white folks had seen to it that his father and mother just died, just left here. He didn't want pity; he didn't even want blood, not the blood out of living bodies. Not the kind of blood white folks understand when they shoot a deaf black man to death, because there are no deer. Not that blood, that you could starve and maim. Leroy wanted the blood of the culture, the songs folks sing, how they move, what they look at, the rhythms of their speech; that was the blood Leroy was after. Blackening up America.

Cypress was blowing kisses to him from across the table, now that they were alone. "I thought you said we had to turn in early."

Leroy slid his tongue to the corner of his mouth so Cypress could barely see it, but would.

"Want some more champagne, 'fore we go home?" she murmured.

Leroy pointed to her crotch. "No, I think there's plenty of champagne up there."

Cypress feigned indignation. "Why sir, that's not very American of you."

Leroy leaned toward her, looking directly into her eyes.

"I'm not a very American guy."

Cypress,

I can't actually tell you why your daddy went to sea. It's real clear there wasn't much work for a skilled Negro carpenter in Charleston, but I figure he never felt at home here on the mainland anyhow. Geechees from the islands don't take to being called foreigners, or made fun of because they have accents.

They weren't the only ones brought from Africa, as you well know, but mainlanders would like to believe that. And years ago folks were much harder on darker members of the race. I suppose he went to sea so he could get away from all that. But don't you go stirring round dry bones, girl. He's laid to rest and peaceable by all accounts. Let it alone.

Leastways, the stories your daddy told you were a world different from anything your little friends heard, and he loved you girls with all his heart. More than that I can't say, because as his wife, I knew him in another way, a private way.

Love,
Mama

P.S. Here's an old photo of your father that I was saving, but you keep it. Maybe he'll make himself clearer to you, if you think on his picture. He's right smart in that outfit, don't you think?

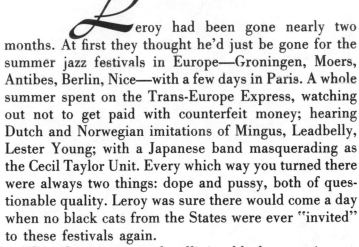

*L*eroy had been gone nearly two months. At first they thought he'd just be gone for the summer jazz festivals in Europe—Groningen, Moers, Antibes, Berlin, Nice—with a few days in Paris. A whole summer spent on the Trans-Europe Express, watching out not to get paid with counterfeit money; hearing Dutch and Norwegian imitations of Mingus, Leadbelly, Lester Young; with a Japanese band masquerading as the Cecil Taylor Unit. Every which way you turned there were always two things: dope and pussy, both of questionable quality. Leroy was sure there would come a day when no black cats from the States were ever "invited" to these festivals again.

"See, Cypress, every headlining black group is on a bill with three or four all-European bands. How long do you think it's gonna take them to say, 'We play just as good as those niggers; we know what they are doing with the music; we don't need to bring them over here any more. We play jazz now.' "

Cypress had laughed till she cried as Leroy mimicked the European producers who were always telling Afro-Americans what they didn't need. " 'Oh, you don't need to rehearse, it's natural with you.' 'Don't bother about accommodations, we have some nice tents and out-houses.' '" But it wasn't funny. Because it was still true that coverage in *Jazz Hot* and *Le Jazz* or records on a French label opened doors that would never open in the States. So Leroy went to Europe.

Cypress fought admitting it, but Leroy had mediated her relationship with the City of New York. She couldn't stand it when he was gone. His horns and his arms had offered her horizons where she was free to see what she chose, feel what she had to, be what she dreamed. Now she was constrained by cement, noise, thousands of people she'd never had to take seriously. Whole blocks of black people without trees. Dance studios that looked into other dance studios. Or vacant lots crammed with tires, garbage, used strollers, broken bottles, and stench. Leroy alone had shielded her from this. Now her land-scape had no natural elements. In California, one was cognizant of the planet: that the earth and sea were forces to contend with. New York without Leroy was bereft of any humility, dwarfing the sun, violating the waters, crowding nature into a yard called Central Park.

Through Mahlon, Cypress discovered alternative landscapes in the middle of Manhattan. Mahlon was a collector. She took Cypress with her to artists' studios, openings, and exhibits. Cypress lived among the bones and Sambos of Betye Saar's altars. She wrapped herself in the gauze and twigs of Gina Hamilton's country vistas. She made magic with the sorceress who haunted Romare Bearden's hills; pried open the cupboards in the shacks where spirit-faces long dead led her in Carolinian nights. Cypress retreated from the shadows of skyscrapers trap-ping the light for the wealthy; she ignored the noises of the City in shadows: people bumping, pummeling one another because they could not see. She danced to McAr-

SUNSHIP JAZZBUNKER

Boomjeskade 11, Rotterdam

vr 10 juni - 10 uur

Leroy McCullough Quintet
& The Butch Morris Trio

FESTIVAL MOERS-DUCS

Pfingsten, im Schlosspark/ 27 mai 18.00 uhr

Joseph Jarman & Roscoe Mitchell
Bobo Shaw & Andrew Cyrille
Leroy McCullough & Baikida Carroll
The Brecker Brothers

Grand Auditorium   lundi
Radio France   13 juillet
FM
France Musique

JAZZ VIVANT/

THE GREAT BLACK MUSIC

l'Art Ensemble de Chicago
et
le Quintette de Leroy McCullough

194/

". . . Leroy McCullough's debut in Europe is the most startling event since John Coltrane worked with Miles Davis. The complexity and rigor of McCullough's compositions force me to wonder where this man, an American Negro, actually comes from . . ."

Guy Sorel, "Revues"
LE JAZZ MODERNE

"Leroy McCullough, saxophonist and composer, broke the humdrum of the evening with accomplished yet fervent solos that played against the pageantry of his group, which is an answer to the contradictions of Sun-Ra, The Art Ensemble, and The Cecil Taylor Unit; throw in some Coleman, Young, Ayler, and every major twentieth-century classical composer, which is to say that McCullough is definitively the most singular of black musicians: a virtuoso. The European jazz scene can only be invigorated by his presence. May France make him welcome . . ."

Juliette Bienaimee,
"La Musique Noir"
CADENCE NOUVELLE

thur Binion's "Drawn Symphony," insisting that she
didn't need to read music, she had climbed into it; over
the hard edges of crayon erupting from aluminum sur-
faces, she'd set up camp and heard Celia Cruz in the
back Mississippi woods, as colored boys denied crayons
made marks on cardboard with sticks, their visions you
could feel. When Cypress went out into the streets, she
donned Mel Edwards' "Five Black Face Images" to
bring the colors of her ancestry to the garment district
in something other than brogands and calloused hands
pushing racks of the latest fashions. What dreams she
found, she moved into. From David Hammons' body
prints that left her trembling, bloody, bound to walls by
her shadows, following her hair wound round branches
weighted down by death, to Barbara Chase-Riboud's
bronze and wool lands, offering her cliffs, ravines, quiet
ponds of braid, paths to reach the other side.

Cypress reconsidered Leroy's easiness in the world.
He wasn't in the world, not like Towbin or Mahlon who
worked in it, not even like Idrina, who forced changes.
Leroy's reality was bounded by his memories of his
father, the flames outside Independence. His horizons
eclipsed the evening news, his version of the world left
the white folks out. Exiles, she and Leroy. They didn't
need to go to Paris; that would do no good. What's the
point of being spat on in France? What could they do
in Rio, where black people are a mythological presence?
No, the frontiers in Leroy's destiny were the sounds he
heard and gave back as music; for Cypress the terrain
of the new world was art. Her dance, like her people
before her, adapted to the contours of her new land. She
choreographed for the wilderness and the metropoli of
the Saars, Binions, and Edwards, who let her have
space, a natural element.

Going up 7th Avenue from the 50th Street local stop
toward that collection of dance schools catering to gyp-

sies, troopers, and novices on the way to Broadway cho-
ruses, regional musicals, and the Folies Bergères in Las
Vegas, Cypress protected herself from hawkers for live
sex shows, 24-hour topless dancers, and cries of "Boys,
boys, boys . . . we got boys," immersed in visions of a
dance. This dance was to take place inside a woven
environment, "Code" by Allen and Dotty Fannin.

Cypress saw three women clad in paisley aprons about
to begin household movements: scrubbing, hanging,
straightening. Then, the Art Ensemble of Chicago's
"Chicongo" would start. The women would resist the
hipness of the rhythms, scrub, hang, and straighten
more intensely, until one began to take on another per-
sonality, that of the lady of the house . . . but a colored
house. Cypress enjoyed commanding this woman's fantasies, her desire to make the others work harder while
she adopted the airs of Hollywood stars. Marlene Die-
trich in *Shanghai Express*. Billie Burke in *Ziegfeld Fol-
lies*. But who the lady of the house was would change
from moment to moment so that all three of the dancers
would interrupt one another's housework, each more
bizarrely grand, grotesque than the others. As the music
faded out, the women were trying to hang, scrub, and
straighten to stop the relentless profanity of women of
leisure; the Busby Berkeley nightmares in mirrors and
kaleidoscopes, idle, coy, and useless. One by one, they
would step out of the closed unspun rayon, drop their
aprons, and become themselves.

Aside from the chores, the movement would be based
in classic images of women from *Giselle* to *Appalachian
Spring*, with Lena Horne in *Stormy Weather*, Eartha Kitt
as herself, and as a Charlestonian, Cypress couldn't
leave out Scarlett O'Hara. The divas of femininity bewitched too many generations, convinced them that the
joys of women were deceit and dependence.

"Hi, sweetheart!" Cypress heard a shout that made

Ntozake Shange

her walk faster. Maybe she was being recruited for one of the blow-job massage parlors. She plunged into the crowd, making diagonals, the shortest distance between two points, etc., but the "Hi, sweetheart" stayed on her ass. At the light she had to wait for a Con Ed truck to make a left turn. Somebody grabbed her shoulder. Cypress turned to knock whoever in the hell it was into the ground, underneath the ground, off the planet, but it was Ariel Moröe of The Kushites Returned, looking like he had been on an excursion in hell.

Several of his front teeth were missing. There were keloids from knife slashes around his eyes, his neck, and upper chest. The twenty pounds he'd lost left his bones peeking through everything he had on, including the skin-tight black leather pants with zippers up the legs. He looked like a middle-aged pixie suffering from anorexia. Cypress couldn't get over the change. Why, Ariel had been so vital, so magnificent in his capes and panache. Talking as if he still had all his teeth, he said,

"Hi, Cypress. We haven't seen you in such a long time. Where you been keeping yourself, girl?"

But Cypress only wanted to know what had happened. "Ariel, what have you done to yourself?" He ignored that, and lit a Sherman.

"We're going back to San Francisco next week. Would really be good to have you back. New York's taken its toll on my first-line soloists."

Cypress thought, "New York's taken its toll on more than your first line, buddy," yet Ariel continued to project into the future, all the wonderful things he'd do when he got his group back to San Francisco. Finally, Cypress blurted, "Ariel, can you still dance? I mean are you strong enough yet?"

"Oh, this." Ariel felt the most protruding scars on his face with his free hand. "Yeah, I'm not where I usedta be, but it's not as bad as it looks, darling."

Cypress felt like slapping him, but she couldn't bring herself to strike anything as fragile as Ariel appeared right then.

"How'd this happen, Ariel? You look awful. My god."

"I made a mistake, that's all. A bad choice of character, you know. I thought he was such a sweet boy, but look . . ." Ariel pulled up the sleeve of his flowered shirt. A hunk of flesh was missing and a hollow shape etched by teeth marks remained. Keloids there, too. Cypress felt nauseous.

"Doggish, huh?" Ariel chimed.

Cypress remembered all those nights in $1.00 cover/2-drink minimum discos and after-hours bars she'd been in with Ariel and his fellas. The quick pick-ups of boys still childlike, yet mean. She saw Ariel fussing over these illiterate, dressed-up hustlers, fawning over them, while they spent his money, snorted his coke. They had laughed at him: "Shut up, old man" . . . "Suck me, old man" . . . "No, honey, let me wear that." Cypress wanted to scream. They had no right; they had no right. Even if Ariel was a fool, thinking anyone could be bought and paid for without some fetid, vicious aftermath, Ariel Moröe was still gifted. He'd trained her to perform; to make her body speak. And now he could barely walk without revealing the cruelty of the company he kept.

Cypress left Ariel on the corner where he'd caught up with her. She had to cut her conversation short when some young thug, in clothes she recognized as Ariel's, sidled up, tapped Ariel on the behind and gave her that "Well bitch, don't you have something to do" look. Cypress moved right on. There was no need to think about The Kushites Returned. The Kushites were destroyed.

Two-thirty jazz class; studio A. Cypress did her warm-ups with a vengeance. She couldn't get away from flashes of Ariel's beating, his wounds, the glory his company had known. She pulled her head toward her knees, through her legs. Stretch. Release. Again. Stretch. Release. And toe-ball-heel, toe-ball-heel. Point. Point.

"On the floor. Ladies. On the floor. Now, off. And one-and-two, and that's it. Pick up the tempo, would you?"

Cypress was working her body so obsessively she didn't realize Idrina was teaching class, until it was time to go across the floor. Idrina called her for the first line, lustily.

"Cypress, give it all you got! Lay-ups into parallel turns as many as you can handle."

Idrina demonstrated. Cypress followed, triumphant. She arched her back to the floor, opening chest, arms reaching for the windows, head at her heel, leg pulling toward the farthest corner. That breath, as all her body expanded in different directions, that moment was for Ariel in his prime. The impulse to turn, catch her shadow still in preparation, was so accurately executed the eloquence forced Idrina to step back. Cypress had learned so well, there was nothing more for Idrina to teach her.

Cypress danced like there was no tomorrow. No kicks were high enough for her; no triplets crisp enough. Why didn't Leroy come home, so she could stop living inside paintings? Why did she have to know Ariel? Or Idrina for that matter, who was apparently smitten with some red-headed wisp of a girl who'd studied ballet too long?

Her emotional circuits overloaded, Cypress pushed her body into street clothes. Her pants wouldn't come over her hips easily; she was still sweating. Her blouse clung to her back like someone chasing her. The day had been too full of old people; people she'd thrown away and let die somewhere nobody would find them, but somehow they came around anyway. Came around full-faced, familiar, and old. Cypress wondered if old memories could make you smell different, make you not know what you were doing. She took deep breaths on a slow ten-beat, and exhaled. In this meditative state, she came upon visions of Mel Edward's "Curtain for William and Peter." She wrapped herself in the delicate barbed wire, winding the chains around her arms. She became a landscape of braided, looped metal, daring some more old, dead, killed-off creatures to cross her path. But some things aren't intimidated by steel and threats to flesh.

Idrina was on the other side of 8th Avenue, enjoying a Sabrett's hot dog with sauerkraut. She did have a few vices. Sabrett's & root beer in the street. That was living in New York, somedays. It was so much more delicious to watch Cypress building moats, sand castles, direct lines to her soul on the corner of 49th Street.

Walking fast, but not without pleasure, Idrina came behind Cypress as she always had, without announcement. Just that sweet tickle round the back of her neck. The smile that offered what could be, whenever Cypress wanted.

"Hi, Cypress. Don't tell anybody I was eating from a street vendor, please. It'll ruin my reputation." Idrina hugged Cypress, who let her barbed wires disintegrate, right there in midtown.

"Oh, Idrina, I'm really glad to see you. I didn't think I would be, but I just saw Ariel. I can't believe what he's done to himself." Cypress held Idrina tight. Idrina caressed her head, soothing this child so willful, they'd never had all they should have.

"Come on, Cypress. I'm gonna take you home. You don't need to be out here in all this." Cypress didn't resist. She knew Idrina wouldn't hurt her, not again. This time they went to Idrina's for comfort, for relief from the loving too much, too many who'd abandoned caring. Some old things lay in wait for the night, deep in citadels where demons play God and memory consecrates our sense of reality. As she slept, Cypress encountered her other worlds, where her scars, fungi, and terrors grew wild.

CYPRESS' DREAM

This was obviously England after a nuclear holocaust. Cypress figured that it must be 2014, at least. Nothing within her view was familiar; the grey was implacable, flat, disrupted only by scurrying women in bright tunics. Some had papers in their hands like secretaries at the stock exchange, others with angular contraptions Cypress felt must be weapons. She was alone in this place, alone in the sense that she didn't "belong," like the rest, to whatever manner of civilization she'd come upon. An impulse to tuck her skirt under her legs—or to throw it off, and far away—came over her body whenever the women with weapons came near. There was something wrong with her appearance, her attitude, though she wasn't sure how or what. She hid in the tubes of shadow along the sides of tunnel after tunnel, curving and neverending, watching the white, brown, and golden women in this world.

Someone found her. Another woman in a red tunic took her to an official place inside the grey world, where she was introduced as a survivor. The leader, the queen, the reigning glory of this community was a tall woman with red hair who welcomed Cypress and kept saying she would be safe. Cypress asked safe from what, thinking that the world might still be at war, but that was only partially the case. After the bombs laid waste to the planet, somehow the men and women of the earth had been separated. "Of course," Cypress thought, "of course." In a war the women are left behind, and the men go away to fight and kill, so when the devastation began and ended, women were left to contend with the fruitlessness of the soils, the weight of the skies. Now each breath meant poison. At any rate, all the women left on the planet had ended up in this cove off Britain; that was many years ago, they said. The men lived somewhere in the Western Hemisphere, plotting and determined to take back their rights to pillage and wreak havoc, but so far the female colony had defended itself against the attackers; violence they claimed was only for self-defense.

Cypress was initiated into the new world—not quite as herself. All vestiges of male-dominated culture were to be "rehabilitated" out of her psyche; the true matriarch, who is the woman-powerful, was to be nurtured. The population wanted for nothing: food, clothing, shelter, or art. These were a woman's work, even in the old world. But here there were no patriarchs, ordering and demanding. Here there were only Mothers and Daughters. "Mothers" were supreme; there was no higher honor than to be deemed "Mother," yet this had nothing to do with biological offspring. Women who had no children were of a higher caste than the "bearers," as they were called. The "bearers" were never seen in public assemblies, nor were they allowed to wear bright colors, because they might bear sons.

The "Daughters" worked in the nurseries, the factories, the offices, the arts, and military of this place where no men were mentioned or seen. Some young girls who pulled Cypress aside to ask her about the other world where men had been present were severely reprimanded; Cypress was instructed by the female guards to watch that she didn't contaminate the young minds with the filth of the past. Immediately after the girls had been scolded, some other brown figure in yellow took her through a passage that became smaller and smaller, until finally Cypress and this woman, Gisa, had to crawl on their stomachs. Eventually, Cypress heard groans, heavy breathings, and screams she recognized as coming from women in labor. Gisa said, "Yes, these are the bearers, our real mothers."

Cypress wanted to stop her, to say, "No. My mother is in Carolina," but she knew her companion wouldn't understand. The "bearers" were in a great black hole that went on for the distance of a football stadium. Cypress thought, "There's no need to put them in a womb; we are the womb," but such a thought was impossible, here. Gisa explained.

"In order to become a bearer, a woman must do something bad: not follow rules; steal; behave strangely."

Cypress couldn't believe it. "You mean giving birth is like a punishment?"

"Yes . . . why else would anyone do it?"

Cypress thought of the fertility pills, the test-tube babies implanted in women's wombs, the invention of surrogate mothers, all the things people of her time did in order to have a baby. Yet, why else would you do it was beyond Gisa's comprehension.

"You know what else they do?" Gisa asked Cypress, who shook her head no. "They murder most of the boy babies. They haven't figured out how to stop that from happening; plus, they don't capture enough men from the outside to keep our population stable, so the boy babies they don't murder, they keep down here and feed them so they can make sperms. Isn't that what you call it, sperms?"

"Uh-huh."

"But once they make the sperms, the Mothers have it frozen, so no one has to worry about touching them," Gisa reassured Cypress, who was longing to touch Leroy, to feel his skin and sinew so this place wouldn't be true.

"But where are they?"

"Why in the gaol, naturally." Gisa smiled, so safe. "Want to go see them? We have to be very careful, 'cause it's against the law . . . if they find us we'll be made bearers."

Cypress wasn't sure she wanted to jeopardize her position in the colony by going to see the men. She'd seen men before; there was not the mystery, like there was for Gisa. Then a curtain opened, and Cypress saw her mother in labor; her very own real mama from Charleston was in the black hole giving birth; and all around her were the female guards carrying small Sassafrasses and Indigoes, toddler-sized Mahlons and Lallahs.

"Oh my god." Cypress caught herself from speaking too loudly. "Oh, Jesus." Most of the "bearers" were black and Latin. "Oh god, not again." Cypress held onto the walls. She was swooning; all of slavery gushing from her stomach.

"That's my mother. I've got to get my mother out."

She kept repeating this while Gisa gently reminded her that they could come back all the time; that no one knew. And Cypress couldn't explain that her people had done this before, filled wombs over and over until they collapsed, or the body let go. Brought children to the soil never to be seen again, bred spirits to be smashed, sold, played with until their connection to the idea of humanity was obliterated. Gisa tried to calm her, leading her further into a black tunnel that opened onto a moat. A huge glass building surrounded by armed guards in purple helmets was in the middle. Cypress could see crocodiles and alligators meandering through the waters. Her skin shuddered. Then she saw them. Boys on the lower levels; young men in the middle levels; old men on the top floors. There was a loud buzz. The men came toward the glass walls that enclosed them, to inject their sperm into individual tubes running the length of the prison.

Cypress thought of all the porno shows she had ever seen or heard of; women masturbating on the stage in front of three hundred men; women hung from trapezes so anyone could eat their pussies for the admission price; women passed around from man to man to be sodomized, cut, beaten. This spectacle belonged with those. Even though no one touched the men, or watched them "perform," the threat of violence, the humiliation, was inherent. Cypress wondered if the boy on the third floor, second cage, was Ariel; he looked like Ariel, and she wanted him out of there. Then she heard one of the guards shout.

"Hurry up, old man. We don't have all day!"

Cypress looked to the highest windowed cage, and there was her father, with his hands behind his back, refusing. Cypress was stunned.

"All right, let him have it," the guard said, and his entire cage crackled with electricity; he was being shocked to submit.

Cypress screamed, "Daddy, Daddy," and a guard came chasing her. It was Idrina, laughing, her father still trapped in the roaring red glow. Cypress whimpered "Daddy . . . Daddy" through the black winding tunnels and caves lined with laughing Idrinas, Ariels jacking off, while the whole colony, alerted to a defector, prepared to capture and punish a felon.

Cypress woke up running; at least, it looked as if she'd been running. Her body hurt like long forced strides, her linen was tossed about like undergrowth round deserted

206/

towns. She was panting, she was sweating. She was crying, hugging herself. Rocking back and forth, shaking her head. No, that wasn't real, there was no such place; that was a dream, everything's all right, now. But everywhere she looked she saw her mother in the cave, giving birth over and over; her father in the electric popping cage, his arms behind his back . . . pain everywhere she turned . . . their faces made ugly for the first time, by something she had dreamed.

Usually she comforted Leroy, who had grabbed her arms from the depths of his sleep that night, trying not to see what he was seeing, yelling "He killed her. He killed her. Towbin's wrong; doesn't understand." Cypress got him to keep talking. "He killed Mama 'cause of that bitch. He killed her."

It had been so hard for Cypress to listen to the ugliness Leroy found in his parents, to reconstruct malignant romantic triangles; lies and longings he'd been trapped in as a boy.

Yeah, he was raised with the best of everything. If it hadn't been for the rigors of any child's life in East St. Louis, he would have been Little Lord Fauntleroy. It wasn't talk about his father and that woman. That was no talk. That was the truth. The nights he spent keeping company with his mama, fixing one last cocktail, until they heard the hum of the Eldorado by the side of the house, confirmed for Leroy that his father had chosen some Guinea bitch young enough to be his daughter, over Eleanora and her geraniums by the picket fence.

Such indiscretions are resolved by little boys when they become men. But Leroy was a man whose dreams told him, "White folks killed your parents, murdered your folks. On account of a piece of ass some white folks murdered your mama. And your pop thought so much of you he let your mama die for his white bitch . . . so

much for the niggers, huh . . . huh?" That's when
Leroy's hands grabbed for Cypress in the night. That's
when Cypress rocked him back and forth, slipping her
fingers through his braids, pushing out the nightmares,
his tears on her thighs. Cypress fought to say, "Let go
of that, Leroy. That's over. Remember the nice things
. . . ," but she wanted to say, "Let's get 'em. Let's make
somebody pay. Somebody has to pay for this."

Now, in contortions she hadn't learned in class, legs
and arms twisted like a dying centipede's, Cypress
vowed on the voices of her dreams; the image of her
mother strapped down and bleeding, her father helpless
in a glass cell. She vowed to avenge her kin. She swore
on the burned limbs of her father and her mother's
smiles stolen from the Charleston swelter that white
folks would not make her ugly, helpless, and lost. She
swore she'd never ask Leroy to remember the nice
things, but to remember all of it. She pulled her head
from beneath the pillows, searching the walls for the
images that terrified her. The faces were still there, but
she was no longer afraid. Idrina wasn't laughing; she lay
still in Cypress' arms.

Cypress laid waste to the tunnels, caverns, and shadows of the other world. She drew upon memories of her
own blood: her presence would be a mortal threat to
those who wounded, maimed, her ancestors, her lovers,
Leroy. Like those women before her who loaded bundles
on their heads and marched off to fields that were not
their own, like the "bearers" of her dreams swamped
with births of infants they would never rear, Cypress
clung to her body, the body of a dancer; the chart of her
recklessness, her last weapon, her perimeters: blood,
muscle, and the will to simply change the world.

My lovely C.,

Did you get the box of costumes I whipped together? I
hope your new company can use them, but pay me next
time, when you're on your feet!

I'm so excited about your association with a national
touring company . . . please, send me clippings, especially
if you play major cities where we have relatives.

You're still in the corps de ballet . . . that's a start.
Nevermind, I'm jumping around so, imagining you in all
those frilly tutus, and your toe shoes . . . you don't know
how happy I am. Plus, the Lord will look kindly on the
benefits you're going to do for Negro Christians; bless your
souls, for taking time from a full season for the race. I'm
mighty proud.

Love,
your Mama

P.S. What's the name of the group—I've been calling you
the American Negro Ballet. I don't like that other group,
Afro-American Ballet . . . who ever heard of such a thing!

"This is the overseas operator. Your call is ready, miss."

"Yes, thank you . . . Leroy, Leroy are you there?"

"Huh?"

"Leroy, it's me, Cypress. I got it. I really got it."

"What, baby . . . jeeze, what time is it there?"

"I don't know, I've been celebrating!"

"What, darling . . . I'm sorta out of it . . . now tell me again."

"Can you hear me?"

"Yes, go on . . . I love you."

"Guess what? I'm in a dance company; I'm going on the road."

"But honey, I'll be back in two weeks."

"Yeah. Yeah, but you can meet me . . . let me see . . . oh, I'm so happy! Why, in two weeks we'll be in Orangeburg, South Carolina."

"What?"

"I'm dancing with this group called Soil & Soul . . . they go all over to raise money and morale . . . bail, legal fees, stuff like that for the Civil Rights Movement."

"But Cypress, the crackers are raising hell out there. You gotta wait for me, 'fore you get yourself killed."

"No Leroy, it's not like that. We travel with the same kinda protection that Rap Brown gets, and the Panther Party, even Ralph Featherstone is on the same circuit . . . don't you understand?"

"Cypress, will you listen to me? What you're talking about is politics; that's not what you're trained to do, is it? Do you know anything about guns, Cypress? Do you know about white folks and bombs? Do you?"

"I know we haveta do something. We promised the shit had to stop here, didn't we? Didn't we say that somebody had to pay?"

"Yes, darling . . ."

"Don't 'yes, darling' me. You're sitting somewhere in France. L'Ouverture's bones should be rattling in your ears, but all you can hear is Europeans being amazed you can read music."

"Cypress, you're being unreasonable."

"Living here is unreasonable, or don't you remember?"

"When do you leave?"

"Day after tomorrow."

"Okay, I'll be there."

"No, you don't haveta come home. I just wanted to tell you what . . . well. I was so proud of myself. Now you made me scream at you . . ."

"Cypress, I'm coming home so I can marry you."

"Oh, Leroy, that's perfect."

"Aren't you supposed to say 'yes'? What do you mean 'Oh, that's perfect'?"

"The first gig is in a church. A church in Valdosta, Georgia."

"That may be where the first gig is, but we're getting married in your mama's house."

"Leroy, are you serious? You want to marry me?"

"I will, if you say yes & stop talking 'bout going to get yourself killed."

"Dancing never killt nobody."

"Dancing in a church in Valdosta might get you blown to bits. Wasn't that the church was bombed a few months ago?"

"Yes, but that's why we have ta keep going back."

Leroy wanted to shake her to her senses, to come cross the waters and kiss her with tides, salt, and the music he heard as she spoke. Pigeons criss-crossed the Tuileries, le Pont Royal, the Louvre; flicks of sunlight waltzed past his windows. Paris was a formidable temptation, but this woman on the other end of the phone was his treasure.

"Listen, Cypress, can Soil & Soul get along without you for a few days?"

"Well, that wouldn't be very professional of me . . ."

"But can they?"

"I guess so . . ."

"Can I get along without you?"

"You been over there for god knows how long . . ."

"Do you want me to get along without you?"

"No."

"Then I'll be back in two days."

"Leroy are we really going to get married in Mama's house?"

"Jesus, Cypress, what do you think I come from? First, I haveta ask for your hand. Then we get the preacher."

"Oh Leroy . . ."

"Don't 'Oh Leroy' me, 'less you gonna give me some."

"You know, I been savin' it for ya."

"Really, is that the truth, now?"

"Darlin', you know what an ol' fashioned girl I am."

Sassafrass had tried everything to be a decent *Ibejii,* a Santera. She desperately wanted to make *Ochá.* To wear white with her *élèkes.* To keep the company of the priests & priestesses. The New World Found Collective where she & Mitch had been living for over a year offered spiritual redemption, if little else. The harvests had been meager so far. Everybody was from cities; never seen a hoe or hay before for that matter. Then, there were the problems of grinding grains, building homes, fetching water, so many things no nationalist dealt with in Newark or Los Angeles.

Mitch just made things harder. Always complaining, refusing to work with the other men, disrespecting the deities, cursing & reminiscing 'bout times that weren't really all that good. Shooting galleries on Main Street. Passing bad bills in Long Beach. The taste of Johnny Walker Black in Watts on a steaming summer night. He wandered from the collective frequently, returning incoherent, dirty, unacceptable.

On the other hand, Sassafrass loved her new life. She made cloth for all the collective, for feasts, for rituals, for sale to tourists come to look at these New Afrikans.

Sassafrass was respected, would have been sought after by men of cleaned spirits had it not been for Mitch.

Mama Mbewe begged her to end this relationship. She threw the cowry shells to see what the spirits saw in the future. She marked Sassafrass with *cacario*, the white chalk, that cleaned evil from the soul. Again & again, Mama Mbewe shook her head slowly, sadly.

"It says you must give up a man. There is a man leading you away from righteousness. A man unfit for the blessings of the spirits."

Sassafrass knew that already. Only two days before the Padrino, Oba Babafumé, had sent her for a live white chicken, which he'd held over her head, before he sent her with 5 fresh oranges & the chicken to throw in moving waters, that Oshun & Shango might come to her aid. Come to her aid, to remove the influence of Mitch, ruled by Elégua & Oya. Mitch had been wearing white for months, not to make *Ochá* (Sainthood), but to curtail his natural instincts.

It'd been useless. Shango's Birthday was approaching. Sassafrass was busy weaving a gigantic red cotton & raffia hanging in His honor. Mitch was nowhere to be seen.

The visiting Padrinos & Madrinas could be heard beginning the rites for Shango's day of birth. *Caboé. Canta para Ebioso. The Abaqua.* Drums & chanting ran thru the lush backwoods of Louisiana. Sassafrass liked to think the slaves would have been singing like that, if the white folks hadn't stolen our gods. Made our gods foreign to us, so the folks in Baton Rouge never came near those "crazy fanatic niggahs" out there.

Mama Mbewe's voice raced thru the forests, the makeshift cabins where weavers, potters, painters, musicians, dancers, and ordinary folks seeking another life had made home.

Sassafrass, Cypress & Indigo

Shango para icoté
Shango para icoté
O de mata icoté
A la ba obaso icoté
A la ba obaso icoté

In the Meeting House Shango's birthday present, a mountain of fresh, unbruised red apples, was in place. An arc of half-smoked cigars smoldered on the ground, a warning or an offering for devotées. In red & white, with *élèkes* or no, the followers added their personal gifts for the deity with the Ax: vials of home-made whiskey, bananas, knives, long-handled axes, brightly colored scarves, shirts, head wraps. Shango was the Warrior who protected The New World Found from marauders, white folks, recidivists. Sassafrass so wanted to be a priestess of Oshun, like Mama Mbewe. To heal, to bring love & beauty wherever she went. This bad spirit on her head confounded all her desires.

Before she went to the Bembée, Sassafrass anointed herself with florida water: a dab on the forehead, under each arm, her navel, her pubic hair, behind each knee, under both arches of her feet. She left glasses full of honey & water in every corner of her cabin. She left bluing by the front door, ammonia at the rear, that no evil should enter her house in her absence. She carried wild flowers with her to offer to Oshun, her Mother, in the event that Oshun, as was her nature, grew jealous during Shango's festivities.

Shango para icoté
Shango para icoté
O de mata icoté
A la ba obaso icoté
A la ba obaso icoté

215/

Shango was Sassafrass' patron, her other father. She knew his birthday was auspicious. Didn't she have bourbon & cigarillos in His honor? Sassafrass tried before anyone saw her to look as if she weren't worried about Mitch. Mitch wasn't in this at all. That's how she tried to look.

The path to the Meeting House was muddy, black, rich. Sassafrass didn't mind the delta mud oozing thru her sandals. She pulled her buba up. Took small steps. Going to meet her Father. Shango & Oshun were her eternal parents, 'sides Hilda Effania & Alfred. She thought her wish might already have been granted, but she went with a request, nonetheless.

Drums, Drums. Drums, welcoming the faithful. Pulling them to move to dance. Shango conquered the forests. All human challengers. When Sassafrass hit the door, the smells overcame her. Incense, smoke, whiskey, rice & beans, lamb curry, honey. Sassafrass fell on her knees in the face of Madrina Mbewe, Mama Kai, Madrina Iyabodé, Madrina Kai, Papa Aklaff, & Padrino Musa, Padrino Obalaji, & Mama Sumara, receiving the *Ibejii*. One by one the followers went to Shango's mountain of apples to pray & reveal their most secret desires. When Sassafrass lay flat on her stomach before Shango's bounty, the seven holy ones laid hands on her. Sassafrass was blessed. She'd risen off the floor. Her body had been seized by Shango, He'd taken her. When the holy ones removed their hands from her shoulders, back, calves, & head, she just lay there, oblivious to everyone. Palms open. Sassafrass prayed that she might have a child. You leave your palms open that the gifts of the gods might have a place in your life.

When Sassafrass could finally move, Mama Mbewe & Mama Sumara assured her that her wish had been granted, but that she'd fall from grace very soon, if she didn't abandon Mitch.

"The new one shall be cursed, if you don't renounce the father. Believe us, he is unclean."

Mitch was in Baton Rouge under all the magnolias, nodding out. Having a grand time, thinking 'bout his first gig with Coltrane, not realizing Trane was dead awready. In the tumult of the Bembée Sassafrass saw Mtume Satá swallow sticks of flames. Shango had chosen him, Shango had given him the gift of eating fire. Madrina Iyabodé whipped thru the celebrants in command of Shango's Ax. She threatened all solid matter. Madrina Kai trembled with such power that no one dared touch her robes. Mitch arrived in his I-been-wearing-these-clothes-since-you-guess-when attire; no one noticed but Sassafrass & the gods. Brothers, from only Shango knows where, surrounded him. The presence of such a mean spirit was forbidden. Mitch, of course, began his usual tirade of "muthafuckah-my-woman-is-in-there." If he'd known she was pregnant, maybe, he'd have acted better. More than likely, if he'd known, he'd have raised more hell.

But he didn't have an opportunity to be a fool or a jackal. No one could stop it. The drummers could only feed her more. The other dancers moved from her path. Sassafrass was in the throes of the wrath of Oshun. How dare you betray me? Her foot stomped. How dare you not recognize my beauty? Her hand brought forth the mirror wherein she admired herself. How dare you make no preparations for my child who is a gift of *las potencias,* the spirits? She grabbed up a jar of honey from Madrina Sumara's hand, danced. Sassafrass danced, tore thru the crowd, spreading honey on the faces, robes, hands of those Oshun chose.

Mitch thought it all very quaint till Sassafrass moved toward him & his saxophone with the weight of Oshun in her step. She pulled gob after gob of honey from Madrina Sumara's glass, stuffed it down the bell of his horn. He still didn't believe. Sassafrass, under Oshun's direction, spread honey from Madrina Kai, Madrina Nashira, Madrina Mbewe all over the horn, till he had the decency to be silent.

Sassafrass wore white. She prayed. She wove cloth, not thinking who it was for. She'd fallen from grace. Mama Mbewe, Mama Sumara, Mama Iyabodé passed chickens over her all night. In the morning, she saw a vision of her Mother. She lay on a bed of oranges, surrounded by burning yellow candles, eating honey. *"I think I'm going to carry these spirits right on home. I guess I live in looms after all. Making things: some cloth and one child, just one."*

Dear Sassafrass,
Of course you can come home! What do you think you could do to yourself that I wouldn't love my girl? As a matter of fact, I believe you and I could go into some kind of business . . . maybe, have a boutique with your weavings that hang and mine that serve useful purposes. (smile)
Now I want you to promise to keep on reading this letter. Right now, before you do another thing. There, you see, you probably look like you used to when you'd done something wrong. Your little mouth would curl under and that lower lip would poke out a wee bit. You poked your mouth different when you were mad. Anyway, I want to say that when girls ask out of the blue sky can they come home, it usually means they're in some kinda trouble. That's why I asked you to promise me you'd keep reading, no matter what. I know you throw out my letters that don't suit your fancy —I birthed you, I know all about you. That's why you're in trouble now, because you took it upon yourself not to listen to your ma. So, as I was saying, if you are in trouble, you just come right on home, quick as you can. There's no time to waste. There's no shame in having made a mistake. Lord knows the history of the race is riddled with mistakes.

Ntozake Shange

Look at that Mitch. Now there's an error if there ever was one. Keep reading. Don't you put this piece of paper down.

You and Cypress like to drive me crazy with all this experimental living. You girls need to stop chasing the coon by his tail. And I know you know what I'm talking about. I swear I am not sure if you would recognize a decent man, if I sent him out there Special Delivery. Politics and good looks do not a decent man make. Mark my words. You just come on home and we'll straighten out whatever it is that's crooked in your thinking. There's lots to do to keep busy. And nobody around to talk foolish talk or experiment with.

Something can't happen every day. You get up. You eat, go to work, come back, eat again, enjoy some leisure, and go back to bed. Now, that's plenty for most folks. I keep asking myself where did I go wrong. Yet I know in my heart I'm not wrong. I'm right. The world's going crazy and trying to take my children with it.

Okay. Now I'm through with all that. I love you very much. But you're getting to be a grown woman and I know that too. You come back to Charleston and find the rest of yourself. (smile)

Love,
Mama

220/

*T*he last time Aunt Haydee opened her mouth, she'd asked Indigo to play some rough blues on that fiddle. That was just before Ella Mae's twins arrived. Indigo'd been rubbing Aunt Haydee's hands on the porch by the scrub pines. The sea breeze left her face loved & clear. Aunt Haydee's hands, the same ones delivered hundreds of brown little babies, yellow tykes, screaming black tiny ol' things, those hands were aching, ugly, unmoving now. Indigo told Aunt Haydee her own stories: how the crocodile got his tail; where the rabbit learned to jump; how the wolf couldn't be trusted. Aunt Haydee rocked in her chair. Now this chair had belonged to Aunt Carrie who was the mother to Aunt Susie Marie whose sister married that half-breed from Allendale, moved all the way to New York City & was killt in a barroom brawl where the Colored carried on.

Ella Mae's delivery was quite ordinary. Everybody came out head first. Nothing was missing on either one. Johnny Orpheus held Ella Mae's left leg, while Indigo raised the right so the babies had a free path. Ella Mae didn't tear. She made a few yells that Christ would have heard in the other world, but Aunt Haydee kept on

murmuring that Ella Mae was a good strong gal, strong
gal, birthing two at a time like this.

"Be proud of yourself, Ella Mae. I ain't never done
none of this. Not a child to my name & I can see whatta
trial you been thru & how the Lord's gonna set a bounty
of goodness upon ya. I can see it, Ella Mae. Don't push
too hard now. Jesus don't want nothing coming express."

Indigo'd studied violin with the white woman Miz
Fitzhugh sent every summer, but she concentrated more
on learning what Aunt Haydee knew. Giving birth, cur-
ing women folks & their loved ones. At first Aunt Haydee
only allowed Indigo to play her fiddle to soothe the
women in labor, but soon the mothers, the children,
sought Indigo for relief from elusive disquiet, hungers
of the soul. Aunt Haydee was no fool. She watched
Indigo playing the fiddle one evening as the tide came
in. It'd been a long time since a colored woman on
Difuskie moved the sea. Some say it was back in slavery
time.

Blue Sunday, that was her name 'cause she was born
on a Sunday & as black as pitch. *Blue Sunday* was the
favorite of Master Fitzhugh, but everytime he came near
her the sea would getta fuming, swinging whips of salt
water round the house where the white folks lived. This
went on for years till *Blue Sunday* was so grown even
Master Fitzhugh knew she'd have to breed or lose him
money. He liked the way her bosom was barely visible,
how her hips defined that coarse scratchy garb field
hands wore. He'd sent her silks, even a corset from
France, but *Blue Sunday*'d tied these round a hog she
left in his library. When he whipped her in fronta all the
slaves before the indigo harvest, all she did was laugh.
No scars, no blood appeared on her back. He threw her
to the overseers, two po' white trash hooligans decent
white folks wouldn't look at. When they were through

with her she was still a virgin. Master Fitzhugh took her, unconscious, to his bed. When he penetrated her, she turned into a crocodile. As a crocodile, *Blue Sunday* was benign. Her only struggle was to remain unconquered. Master Fitzhugh was left with one leg, but otherwise quite himself. The Fitzhughs no longer cultivated indigo as a cash crop. *Blue Sunday* was never seen again by any white person, but women of color in labor called on her and heard her songs when they risked mothering free children.

Now this is what the folks said. What actually transpired when the sea was rough & a woman was in labor was that Aunt Haydee pleaded with *Blue Sunday* to "Please, give this child life, please, give this child the freedom you know." Then Indigo would play her fiddle, however the woman wanted. Once Hilda Effania came to get Indigo after Sister Liza Anne had been in labor for 48 hours, but Indigo'd fiddled her own mother out the cabin. There was nothing could come between Indigo, Aunt Haydee, & new people of color. Hilda gave up. Miz Fitzhugh gave up. When Aunt Haydee died, right after Ella Mae's twins first suckled, Indigo just picked up her fiddle. Aunt Haydee went to Our Lord on a melody only Indigo or *Blue Sunday* could know.

Johnny Orpheus tried to give Indigo a few dollars for his two boys, Muhammed & Ali, but Indigo declined. She'd lost Aunt Haydee, which meant we'd all lost touch with a thirst for freedom. Indigo would have tossed Aunt Haydee's ashes to the waves sauntering up to the cabin every now & then, but she decided to carry Aunt Haydee home in a funny bluish jar Uncle John'd given her when she was small. Uncle John had told her that colored trapeze artists usedta spit into that jar or be strung up by their heels. Now that was a long time ago, but that's what he said.

No one had ever expected it, but that child from

Charleston, that Indigo, moved into Aunt Haydee's tabby hut, just like she belonged there. It wasn't that she didn't have gifted hands or a tenderness that could last a lifetime. It was just folks weren't sure where she came from or how she came to be among them. Charleston was far away.

Indigo knew, holding Aunt Haydee's ashes in her arms, she'd not be back for a long while. Charleston wasn't her home, any more than *Blue Sunday* hadn't suffered. In Martinique with the other black people, Indigo could have carried her aunt's ashes on a ferry, but 'tween Difuskie & Charleston she was lucky to be on more than a canoe.

She spent little time on it, but she was concerned. Her sisters were artists. Would they understand she just wanted where they came from to stay alive? Hilda Effania knew Indigo had an interest in folklore. Hilda Effania had no idea that Indigo was the folks.

Somebody said that the day Indigo left Difuskie, 2,000 *Blue Sundays* came out dancing to Scott Joplin, drinking moonshine, & showing their legs. Indigo never denied this, but she kept a drawer fulla silk stockings that had not a run, & she'd never been one to miss a dance, when the aqua-blue men strode up from the sea, the slaves who were ourselves.

*H*ilda Effania couldn't think of enough to cook. She couldn't even clean anything else in her house. She looked at Alfred's portrait over the parlor fireplace, a little embarrassed.

"You know, Al, I did the best I could, but I don't think they want what we wanted."

"Now, Sassafrass. This ain't nothin' but a baby. You think you the only one ever did this?" Indigo coached. "Push I say, don't act a fool!"

"Mama did this three times. God is asking you for one time. One time make a free child." Cypress massaged.

"Yes, darlin'. I'm here. Was there ever one time when you couldn't come home? Yes, darlin', I know this isn't the way you wanted. But, sweetheart, whoever you are is all we have & I swear for Jesus, you my child."

Mama was there.